Widow's Web

Markus Matthews

Published by Markus Matthews, 2024.

This is a work of fiction. Similarities to real people, places, or events are entirely coincidental.

WIDOW'S WEB

First edition. November 3, 2024.

Copyright © 2024 Markus Matthews.

ISBN: 979-8227383105

Written by Markus Matthews.

The Widow's Web

The invitation arrived on a quiet Tuesday, thick parchment sealed with crimson wax, addressed in looping script that felt more like a whisper than a greeting. Mara Fenton could hardly remember the last time she had seen such an envelope, let alone received one. But when she pried it open, her curiosity turned to disbelief. She had inherited Blackwood Manor, a vast, secluded estate tucked away in the mist-laden countryside, from a woman she had never met—a woman who had apparently been watching her for years.

The widow, as the letter referred to her, had left no other family and had chosen Mara, a distant relative at best, to carry on her legacy. The words were delicate and warm, almost pleading. Yet, something about them felt wrong. Perhaps it was the peculiar phrasing that hinted at unfinished business, or the ink that seemed to shimmer like the edge of a shadow.

Against her better judgment, Mara felt compelled to accept, drawn by something she couldn't explain—a strange urgency, like a string tightening around her wrist. She travelled alone to the isolated manor, nestled within a valley that seemed carved from the edge of another world. When she first saw the manor, with its twisted iron gates and looming stone walls, she sensed its secrets waiting to be unearthed.

But this inheritance came with rules, strange and forbidding. She was to keep to the west wing, lock her door at night, and—above all—never disturb the east wing, the part of the house where the widow had once lived and died.

It wasn't long before Mara felt the walls of the house closing around her, a feeling of being watched, of being weighed and judged. Footsteps echoed in empty corridors, and whispers from unknown rooms reached her ears, fragments of secrets she was warned never to uncover. Shadows moved in the corners of her vision, and the eyes in the portrait of the widow seemed to follow her every step. Each night, the tension grew, as if the house itself had a pulse that matched her racing heart.

Now, as Mara delves deeper into the widow's life and uncovers the tragedies that haunt Blackwood Manor, she realizes that this inheritance is not a gift—it is a trap. Bound by blood, she is forced to unravel a mystery laced with betrayal, obsession, and vengeance. But as the shadows close in and the house reveals its darker nature, Mara begins to wonder if she can survive this web of despair—or if she, too, will become another lost soul in the widow's web.

Part I: The Invitation
Chapter 1: The Summons

Mara Fenton wasn't used to receiving mail, much less mail that bore the kind of strange weight this one did. The envelope was thick, heavy in her hands, crafted from some kind of creamy, expensive parchment that hinted at an era when letters meant more than quick exchanges or promotional offers. Her name was written in a curling script across the front—"Miss Mara Fenton"—with a precision that seemed both refined and oddly familiar, though she couldn't place why.

The day had been a strange one already. There was something about the air, thick and slow, like the moment before a thunderstorm broke. The morning light had been golden and hazy, and now, in her small city apartment, Mara felt its waning warmth through the slats of her blinds. She set the letter on her counter and stared at it, feeling an absurd sense of hesitation. It had no return address, no indication of who might have sent it.

It took her another moment, but finally, she picked up the letter and broke the wax seal—a deep crimson stamp of unfamiliar design. As she unfolded the thick, crisp paper within, her eyes scanned the lines of elaborate handwriting.

To Miss Mara Fenton,

I am pleased to inform you of a matter of inheritance.

You are named as the primary beneficiary of Blackwood Manor, an estate owned and maintained by your distant relation, Mrs. Seraphina Blackwood. Mrs. Blackwood, who recently passed, specified in her will that the manor and its surrounding properties were to be offered to you upon her death. You are invited to visit the property at your convenience to accept the inheritance and, if it is your wish, assume ownership.

The house and land hold a significant legacy, and Mrs. Blackwood expressed a hope that her sole remaining kin would carry forth that legacy. It is important to note that this is not merely an invitation but a formal summons. It is, perhaps, your destiny to assume this role.

Upon arrival, please make yourself known to the caretaker, Mrs. Lydia Havers, who will provide you with further instructions and answer any questions you may have about the property.

I look forward to welcoming you to Blackwood Manor.

Yours faithfully, Edgar Lowe, Esq.

Mara's gaze lingered on the name "Mrs. Seraphina Blackwood." The name was unfamiliar, a shadow at the edge of memory, as if she'd once overheard it in a half-forgotten conversation. The idea of "inheritance" left her uneasy, but also, unexpectedly, curious. She'd always known her family history was complicated, a patchwork of thin connections and foggy relations that stretched across countries and centuries. Her parents had passed young, and her grandparents hadn't spoken much about their lineage. Whoever Mrs. Seraphina Blackwood was, she had certainly not been part of Mara's life.

"Blackwood Manor," she muttered, as if saying the name aloud might bring her some clarity. But the name felt foreign and strange, like a storybook she'd never read. For a long moment, she sat there, rolling it around in her mind, wondering what kind of place could harbour a legacy she'd never known.

The letter didn't specify where the manor was, but with some quick research, she discovered it was in an isolated part of the countryside, hundreds of miles from her city life. It seemed more like a scene from an old gothic novel than a real place. Remote, surrounded by vast forests and secluded enough to be cut off from nearby villages, Blackwood Manor was the kind of estate that spoke of history, age, and a certain kind of grandeur that hinted at long-kept secrets.

She tried to imagine it, but all she could conjure was an imposing silhouette, an old manor shrouded in mist, forgotten by time. She felt a shiver, something prickling just beneath her skin—a strange sensation that she wasn't sure was anticipation or anxiety.

Inheritance. It was a peculiar word, conjuring ideas of belonging and responsibility she hadn't given much thought to before. But more than that, it was the letter's peculiar phrasing—It is, perhaps, your destiny to assume this role—that unnerved her. Who talked like that? And what kind of inheritance came with so much weight?

She scanned the letter again, noting the name "Mrs. Lydia Havers," the caretaker. So, this estate had been cared for, preserved, not left to decay with its owner's death. Someone was expecting her. The realization gave her an odd, lingering feeling of both obligation and dread.

For a moment, Mara thought about dismissing the entire notion. What did she need with an estate? She had her life here, her work, her routine. She was independent, though she often felt rootless, a feeling she'd grown used to. Blackwood Manor felt like a disruption. It had the weight of something old, something that might pull her into its web, a spider's invitation.

Yet even as she debated, Mara felt an odd, inexorable pull. It was as if some invisible hand had reached through the pages and pressed into her chest, urging her forward. Blackwood Manor, she thought, might be the answer to questions she hadn't dared to ask. In a family with so many missing pieces, maybe this was one of them.

She folded the letter carefully and tucked it back into its envelope, feeling the faintest twinge of excitement mixing with her unease. She knew she could ignore it, throw it away, bury it under the stack of other unopened mail on her counter. She could pretend the letter had never arrived, continue on with her life, untouched and unbothered by mysterious letters or imposing estates.

But she knew she wouldn't do that. Deep down, Mara realized she would go. She would see Blackwood Manor, walk its halls, perhaps put together some pieces of the puzzle of her family history. And, if nothing else, she might finally feel that root she had longed for—something tying her to the past, giving her some sense of place.

In the coming days, she packed a small bag, booked a train ticket, and prepared for the journey, her mind flickering between images of a strange estate, shadowy halls, and a history she didn't yet know. Her curiosity wrestled with her hesitation as she read and re-read the letter until every word was committed to memory.

But beneath that anticipation was a faint, unsettling feeling—a whisper of something darker, something reaching from that place to pull her in.

Chapter 2: The Threshold

The sky had turned a steel-grey by the time Mara arrived, clouds hanging low and thick like some vast, oppressive ceiling. A fine drizzle misted the air, dampening her face and soaking into the fibres of her coat as she stepped out of the car, the gravel crunching beneath her boots. In front of her, Blackwood Manor loomed, its dark stone facade casting a shadow over the winding path she'd just taken up the hill. The manor was vast, every corner and tower twisted into intricate, sharp edges that seemed to scrape at the sky. Ivy clung to the walls, creeping up like skeletal fingers, as if the earth itself were trying to pull the house back into its depths.

There was an eerie stillness about the place. Not a single leaf stirred in the skeletal branches of the trees that lined the path, and no birds sang. It was as if the house held its breath, watching her arrival with some kind of silent expectation. For a moment, Mara wondered if she was truly alone here, or if the house itself had a presence, waiting to reveal itself once she dared cross its threshold.

She barely had time to take it all in before she heard the crunch of footsteps. From the shadows near the front door, a figure stepped forward—an older woman, bundled against the chill in a dark, heavy coat. Her grey hair was neatly pinned back, and she moved with the practiced care of someone who had lived in a place like this for decades. Her expression, however, was hard to read, a mixture of politeness and something more guarded.

"You must be Miss Fenton," the woman said, her voice a little hoarse, yet carrying an authority that echoed across the empty courtyard.

"Yes," Mara replied, her own voice sounding small against the manor's towering walls. "And you must be Mrs. Havers?"

The woman nodded. "Lydia Havers, caretaker of Blackwood Manor. It's a pleasure to meet you, though I wish it were under... different circumstances."

Mara sensed a pause, as if Mrs. Havers had hesitated to say more, but before she could press, the woman gestured toward the door.

"Come inside, miss. It's not a night to linger out here." She offered a thin smile, though her eyes held no warmth. "The house can feel a bit imposing at first, but you'll get used to it soon enough."

Mara wasn't sure if "getting used to it" was something she wanted. But she followed Mrs. Havers, stepping over the threshold and into the dim, cavernous entrance hall. Inside, the manor seemed even larger, a great expanse of dark wood and cold stone stretching up to a shadowed ceiling that she couldn't quite make out in the faint light. A grand staircase twisted upward in front of her, its carved banister worn with age, leading into a yawning darkness above. The air was thick and heavy, tinged with a faint scent of dust and something else—a smell she couldn't quite place, like damp earth after rain, mingled with a strange, metallic sharpness.

Mrs. Havers led her deeper into the house, her footsteps echoing against the cold floor. Mara glanced around, taking in the details of the entrance hall: the intricate carvings along the walls, the wrought iron fixtures, and the immense, looming shadow of the staircase that seemed to watch her with a silent patience. She felt small here, dwarfed by the sheer size and age of the place, as if it held memories she would never be able to understand.

"Mrs. Havers," Mara began hesitantly, "I don't know much about Blackwood Manor or its history. I only recently found out I was related to Mrs. Blackwood. Is there anything I should know about... about this place?"

Mrs. Havers stopped and turned, fixing Mara with a look that was difficult to read. There was something in her gaze—caution, perhaps, or maybe even reluctance. She clasped her hands in front of her, and for a moment, Mara thought she might refuse to answer altogether.

"The manor is... old," Mrs. Havers said finally, her voice quiet. "It's seen a great deal over the years, but perhaps some things are best left in the past. Mrs. Blackwood was the last of the Blackwood line, a woman of... complex dispositions." She paused, glancing around the hall as if ensuring no one was listening. "But she kept this place intact, as it was meant to be."

A silence stretched between them, thick and uncomfortable. Mara wanted to ask more, but something in Mrs. Havers' manner told her the questions might go unanswered, at least for now.

"I understand," Mara said instead, though she felt anything but understanding. The weight of the place was almost tangible, like an unspoken story hovering in the air.

Mrs. Havers nodded approvingly. "Good. It's best to start slowly here. I've prepared a room for you in the west wing, where you'll find most of the rooms for daily use." She gestured toward a side hallway that led away from the main staircase. "The east wing... well, it's not in use."

Mara hesitated, sensing there was more to that statement than Mrs. Havers was willing to explain. She glanced toward the east wing, which disappeared into shadows, its door closed and imposing. "Not in use?" she repeated, letting the words linger in the air.

Mrs. Havers pressed her lips together, her expression unreadable. "It's best to leave certain rooms undisturbed. Mrs. Blackwood... valued her privacy."

The way she said it sent a chill down Mara's spine, but she didn't press further. Instead, she allowed Mrs. Havers to lead her through the maze of hallways, trying to keep track of the twists and turns but quickly losing her sense of direction in the labyrinthine layout of the house. The halls were dimly lit, only a few wall sconces casting an eerie, flickering light that seemed to exaggerate every shadow. Along the walls, there were empty spaces where it looked as though paintings or mirrors had once hung, but now only the faint outlines remained, their absence leaving the walls strangely bare.

As they walked, Mara noticed odd details here and there—a set of stairs that led up to a door that was firmly locked, a tall grandfather clock that chimed quietly despite its hands showing no time, and peculiar scratches along the walls, as if someone had tried to claw their way through.

Eventually, they reached her room—a modest yet elegant space, with high windows draped in thick, heavy curtains, a four-poster bed, and a small fireplace, its coals dimly glowing. The room felt at once welcoming and stifling, the warmth of the fire unable to chase away the faint chill that clung to the air.

Mrs. Havers set down Mara's bag beside the bed and turned to her. "If you need anything, I'm nearby. My quarters are on the ground floor, just past the main staircase. But I would advise you to lock your door at night. It's an old house, and... strange things can happen."

There it was again—that strange hesitance, as though Mrs. Havers wanted to say more but held herself back. Mara felt her skin prickle. "Strange things?" she repeated.

Mrs. Havers smiled, but it was thin and humourless. "Old houses have their quirks. You'll grow accustomed to them in time." She turned to leave, but paused at the door, her hand resting on the doorknob. "And Miss Fenton... it is wise to heed the house rules."

With that, she left, closing the door softly behind her, leaving Mara alone with the flickering fire and the weight of Mrs. Havers' warnings pressing down on her.

The silence thickened as soon as the door clicked shut. Mara glanced around the room, noting how the shadows seemed to stretch across the walls, moving with the uncertain light of the fire. Despite the warmth of the flames, a chill settled deep in her bones, a feeling that went beyond the cold of the stone walls and into something deeper, something that felt almost like a warning.

She sat on the edge of the bed, the old wood creaking beneath her. Her gaze drifted to the door, and after a moment's hesitation, she got up and locked it, her mind buzzing with questions and an unsettling sense of anticipation. For now, the door was a barrier, a small assurance against the strangeness of the house.

But as she lay down and the quiet of the manor settled around her, Mara couldn't shake the feeling that she had crossed a threshold that she might never be able to return from, that Blackwood Manor had drawn her in, and that somewhere, in its hidden depths, something was waiting.

Chapter 3: The Widow's Portrait

The morning came shrouded in fog, casting Blackwood Manor in a pallid, ghostly light that seeped through the cracks around Mara's heavy curtains. She had slept fitfully, waking several times to the unfamiliar creaks and whispers of the old house, her heart pounding in the stillness. Each time, she would strain her ears, listening to the silence until sleep took her again. The unease of the night still lingered as she dressed, and though she was eager to explore, she felt a growing sense of caution.

After a brief breakfast alone in the dining room—Mrs. Havers nowhere to be seen—Mara set off down the maze-like hallways of the manor. She wanted to see more of the house, to understand the strange place that had become hers by fate or inheritance. The west wing was mostly empty, its rooms filled with old, forgotten furniture covered in sheets, a few cold fireplaces, and a sparse collection of books and artifacts gathering dust.

It wasn't until she turned a corner near the main staircase that she saw it.

There, looming over the hallway, was an enormous portrait, its frame dark and heavy, as if crafted from the very shadows that filled Blackwood Manor. The painting seemed to dominate the space, its presence imposing and unmistakable. Mara felt a chill travel down her spine as she approached it, her eyes drawn inexorably to the figure within.

The woman in the portrait was dressed in mourning black, her gown rich with detail, almost luxurious, but severe in its style. She was seated in an ornate chair, her hands folded delicately in her lap. A veil of sheer black lace covered her hair, and her eyes, dark and piercing, stared out from beneath it with an intensity that seemed to follow Mara's every movement. There was a strange, almost ghostly quality to her face—high cheekbones, lips that barely curved, and eyes that held a mysterious sadness, tinged with something darker, a kind of solemn authority that sent a shiver through Mara.

Though Mara had never seen this woman before, she knew instinctively who she was.

The Widow.

Seraphina Blackwood.

The figure in the painting seemed to radiate a presence, an energy that filled the hall. Mara found herself frozen before it, captivated and unnerved, as if the woman in the portrait were waiting for her to speak, to explain herself, perhaps even to offer some kind of apology for intruding upon her space. The longer she looked, the more she felt that the woman's expression shifted, subtly but unmistakably, a flicker of movement in the eyes that was surely impossible.

"Mrs. Blackwood..." she whispered, the words escaping her before she could stop them.

The moment she spoke, a chill seeped into the room, brushing across her skin. Mara blinked, feeling the weight of the portrait settle on her, as if it were drawing her into the manor's dark history. She tore her gaze away, her pulse quickening, and took a step back. But no matter how she moved, the widow's eyes seemed to follow her, those dark, unreadable eyes penetrating her with silent judgment.

"Beautiful, isn't she?"

Mara jumped, her heart racing as Mrs. Havers appeared beside her, emerging from the shadows with a quiet grace that was almost unsettling.

"I didn't hear you," Mara murmured, her voice shaky. "I was just... admiring the portrait."

Mrs. Havers looked at the painting with a strange expression, her gaze holding a flicker of something Mara couldn't quite place—perhaps respect, perhaps something closer to fear.

"That's the Widow Blackwood," Mrs. Havers said, her voice low, almost reverent. "She was the last of the Blackwood's, before her passing. She lived here alone for many years after her husband's death, guarding the estate and... its secrets."

"Secrets?" Mara echoed, her curiosity piqued. But Mrs. Havers didn't answer right away, her eyes fixed on the portrait with an intensity that matched the widow's gaze.

"She was a complicated woman," Mrs. Havers continued, her words careful. "People say the house took on her spirit after she passed, as if her presence lingered in the walls. Some believe she never really left."

The words settled uneasily in Mara's mind, like a stone dropping into dark water. "What do you mean?"

Mrs. Havers finally tore her gaze away from the portrait, her expression guarded. "Blackwood Manor has always been a place of mystery, Miss Fenton. It was said that Mrs. Blackwood kept to herself, that she held strange beliefs and practiced certain... rituals. She was rumoured to have an affinity for things most people couldn't understand." She paused, then added in a quieter tone, "It's best to respect her memory. Her presence remains part of this house."

Mara's eyes drifted back to the portrait. The widow's expression seemed to shift again, the faintest hint of a smile now haunting her lips, as if she were amused by the conversation unfolding in front of her. The idea of Seraphina Blackwood lingering in the halls, watching from the shadows, unsettled Mara deeply, but it also stirred something in her—a sense of intrigue, a need to understand this woman who had, in some way, summoned her here.

"Did you know her?" Mara asked, turning to Mrs. Havers, hoping for some glimmer of understanding.

Mrs. Havers' gaze hardened slightly. "I served her in her final years. She was a private woman, very particular. I respected her wishes, as any loyal caretaker should."

There was a finality to her tone that warned Mara against pressing further. Mrs. Havers was clearly a gatekeeper to the secrets of Blackwood Manor, but she had no intention of giving them up freely.

For a moment, Mara considered asking her directly about the rumours—the whispers of hauntings and rituals, the strange pull the house seemed to exert—but she held back. The atmosphere around them felt heavy, as if the house itself were listening, waiting to see how much she dared to ask.

Instead, she took one last look at the widow's portrait, feeling a shiver run through her. The woman in the painting had the look of someone who knew far too much, someone who could see beyond the veil of the present and into something darker, something buried deep within the manor's walls. Her gaze held a strange power, a warning, perhaps, or even an invitation.

The fog outside thickened, pressing against the windows and casting the room in an eerie grey light. Mara felt the weight of the widow's eyes even as she turned to leave, and it stayed with her as she followed Mrs. Havers down the hall.

As they walked, she felt an inexplicable urge to look back, to glance once more at the painting. But she resisted, sensing that to look back would somehow give in to the widow's silent call, acknowledging the hold she already seemed to have over Mara.

"You'll become accustomed to it in time," Mrs. Havers said as they moved away, her voice almost sympathetic. "Everyone does."

But Mara wasn't so sure. The widow's gaze, her presence, felt like something that would never truly let go.

Chapter 4: The House Rules

That afternoon, as the grey light faded to a dull dusk, Mara sat with Mrs. Havers in the small, dimly lit sitting room. The fire crackled weakly, casting flickering shadows on the walls, and the air felt thick with something Mara couldn't quite place—a sense of foreboding that hung over the room like a shroud. Mrs. Havers poured them both tea from an ancient, tarnished silver pot, her movements careful and precise. She glanced at Mara with a solemn expression, her lips pursed as though she had something important—perhaps unsettling—to say.

"There are a few things you must know about Blackwood Manor," Mrs. Havers began, her voice low and steady. She folded her hands in her lap, fixing Mara with an intense gaze. "This house is old, and its rules are as much a part of it as the stones and mortar. It would be wise of you to remember them."

Mara felt a prickle of unease, a sense that these were not the ordinary house rules of polite society but something stranger, something that carried the weight of hidden history.

"What rules?" she asked, setting her teacup down, her fingers unconsciously curling into her palms.

Mrs. Havers took a measured breath, her eyes never leaving Mara's. "First and foremost," she began, "you are not to enter the east wing."

Mara's brows knit in confusion. She had glimpsed the east wing only briefly upon her arrival, noticing the way it disappeared into shadows. Even then, something about it had seemed... off, as if it held secrets too dark to be disturbed.

"Why not?" Mara asked, trying to sound casual, though her curiosity was unmistakable.

Mrs. Havers' gaze sharpened. "The east wing was Mrs. Blackwood's private quarters, and she was very particular about her privacy, even in death. Some places in this house are best left undisturbed." She paused, her tone turning grave. "It's... safer that way."

Mara's skin prickled with an instinctive apprehension. Safer. The word lingered in the air, weighted and ominous, as if the house itself harboured an unspoken warning. She nodded slowly, though the restriction only fuelled her curiosity.

"Second," Mrs. Havers continued, "you must keep all doors locked at night."

Mara blinked, surprised by the odd rule. "Locked? Every door in the house?"

"Yes," Mrs. Havers replied firmly. "Lock your bedroom door and any other doors in the west wing you might have opened during the day. There are... movements in the night. This house has a way of shifting, almost as if it breathes. Locked doors help keep it in check."

Mara felt a chill creep up her spine. Movements in the night. She wanted to ask what exactly Mrs. Havers meant by that, but the older woman's expression was stony, almost as if daring her to press for more. Instead, Mara nodded, feeling the weight of these peculiar instructions settle in her mind.

"And lastly," Mrs. Havers said, her voice dropping to a near-whisper, "you are never to go into the attic."

The way she said it was almost like an invocation, each word heavy and final. Mara's gaze flicked upward, as if she could somehow glimpse the attic through the many floors above them. She hadn't given much thought to the attic, hadn't even known it existed, but now it loomed large in her mind, a place of mystery shrouded in shadows.

"Why the attic?" Mara asked, keeping her voice steady despite the unease settling over her. "Is there something dangerous up there?"

Mrs. Havers' mouth drew into a thin line, her eyes distant. "The attic is... where certain things were kept," she said, her tone careful and measured. "Over time, Mrs. Blackwood collected items—objects of power and history, things that were not meant for the hands of ordinary folk." She paused, then added, "The attic is a place of rest, but not a peaceful one. Disturbing it... would not be wise."

Mara swallowed, her curiosity warring with a growing sense of dread. Each rule seemed more cryptic than the last, leaving her with more questions than answers. Yet there was something in Mrs. Havers' demeanour, a quiet insistence that made her hesitant to challenge these restrictions.

"What happens if I don't follow the rules?" she asked softly, her voice barely above a whisper.

Mrs. Havers' gaze turned cold, a flicker of something almost like fear passing across her face. "Disregarding the house rules has consequences," she said, her tone stern. "Blackwood Manor is... sensitive. It has endured much, and it remembers everything. The house holds its own, and those who disrespect it often find themselves regretting it."

Mara's stomach twisted as the words sank in. There was something ominous in Mrs. Havers' voice, a suggestion that the house was more than just stone and wood—that it had a will of its own, a need to protect its secrets. It was as though the manor were alive, an ancient, slumbering creature waiting to react to any slight against its rules.

"I understand," Mara replied, though she could hardly make sense of what she was agreeing to.

Mrs. Havers nodded approvingly, but her eyes held a warning, a silent plea to heed these rules. She leaned forward slightly, her voice dropping even lower, as if what she was about to say were a forbidden secret.

"Mrs. Blackwood was a woman of... intense beliefs," she said slowly. "She practiced certain rituals, things that went beyond the ordinary. This house became a vessel for her—her grief, her anger, her obsessions. It holds on to her still. The rooms... the walls... they are steeped in her memory. It is best to tread carefully."

Mara felt a shiver run through her. The words hung in the air, filling the room with a palpable tension. It was as if Mrs. Havers had unveiled a hidden layer of the house, revealing not just rules but a legacy of secrets, a history that seeped into every corner of Blackwood Manor.

"Thank you, Mrs. Havers," Mara said finally, her voice barely audible. "I'll be careful."

Mrs. Havers nodded once more, her expression softening just slightly. "That's all I ask, Miss Fenton. Respect the house, and it may yet respect you in return."

With that, she rose, signalling the end of the conversation. Mara watched as she left, her footsteps echoing down the hall until they faded into silence.

Left alone, Mara felt the weight of the house pressing down on her. The rules—no entry to the east wing, locked doors at night, and a strict prohibition on the attic—seemed less like instructions and more like warnings. They were boundaries, set not just to maintain order but to contain something within the house, to keep certain forces at bay.

Her gaze drifted around the room, to the shadowed corners, the dusty shelves, the silent walls. For the first time, she felt as though the house were watching her, studying her reaction to the rules, waiting to see if she would abide by them.

As night fell and Mara prepared to return to her room, she remembered Mrs. Havers' words: Movements in the night. She felt a chill as she slid the bolt across her bedroom door, hearing the faint click of the lock echo in the silence. It was just a precaution, she told herself, but the tension in her shoulders told her otherwise.

Lying in bed, Mara stared at the ceiling, her thoughts racing through everything Mrs. Havers had said. Somewhere in the darkened house, the east wing sat shrouded in mystery, the attic lay sealed and restless, and shadows moved in the night, just beyond the locked doors. Each rule felt like a piece of an intricate puzzle, a map of boundaries that she could sense but not yet understand.

As she drifted off to sleep, Mara felt the quiet of the house settle over her, the air thick with secrets she could almost taste. She knew that her arrival had stirred something in Blackwood Manor, something that had been dormant, perhaps even waiting.

And as she lay there, on the edge of sleep, she could have sworn she heard the faintest sound from beyond her locked door—a whisper, a rustle, as if someone, or something, were just outside, watching her, testing the boundaries she had been so carefully warned to keep.

The house had its rules. And Mara was beginning to understand that breaking them would come at a cost.

Chapter 5: Strange Sounds

The first night Mara had locked her door, she'd done so with a tinge of reluctance, feeling the rule more unnecessary than ominous. But tonight, with Mrs. Havers' warnings fresh in her mind, she bolted it with a firm hand, checking it twice before retreating to bed. She lay there for some time, listening to the silence around her. It was an expectant silence, thick and heavy, like the house was holding its breath.

She had begun to drift into sleep when she heard it—a faint, rhythmic tapping, muffled and distant, barely audible. Her eyes flew open, her senses suddenly sharp. It could be anything, she told herself. Old houses made sounds, especially ones as ancient as Blackwood Manor. It was probably the wooden beams settling, the floors shifting, or perhaps even a draft stirring something loose in one of the old rooms.

The tapping continued, unhurried and oddly deliberate. It would stop for a few moments, then resume, each tap separated by an unnervingly long pause, as if someone—or something—were waiting for her reaction. Mara lay perfectly still, her breath shallow as she strained to listen. The tapping echoed faintly through the walls, traveling down the long, empty corridors and seeping into her room.

Just as she was beginning to convince herself it was nothing, the sound changed.

It grew closer.

The tapping was no longer muffled but sharp, distinct, as if it were moving steadily down the hallway outside her room. Her heartbeat quickened as she listened, each tap a slow, measured step that crept closer with each passing second. There was a lightness to it, a skittering quality that reminded her of nails against wood, or perhaps a cane rhythmically striking the floor.

Her mind raced. Perhaps Mrs. Havers was still awake, moving through the halls, checking the doors as she did each night. Perhaps it was just her, fulfilling her duties as the house's keeper. But then she remembered the firm set of Mrs. Havers' instructions: Lock your door at night.

The sound paused just outside her room. She held her breath, her ears straining in the thick silence, waiting for any indication of what was causing the noise. Then, just as suddenly, she heard a faint whisper, a voice so quiet it was barely more than a breath, hissing against the wood like a faint draft.

It wasn't words, exactly—just an indistinct murmur, a flow of sounds and syllables that sent a chill through her. She couldn't understand it, but there was something unnerving about its rhythm, an almost hypnotic quality that seemed to wind its way into her mind. She pressed herself deeper into her bed, her heart pounding so loudly she was sure it would betray her presence.

The whispering grew softer, then louder again, like someone speaking just on the other side of the door, their voice moving closer, retreating, then returning again. She had never felt this kind of dread before, a cold, gripping fear that made her muscles tense and her skin prickle with an almost electric charge.

The tapping resumed, louder this time, echoing just outside her door. Each tap seemed to vibrate through the floorboards, almost as if in sync with her heartbeat. She stared at the door, half expecting to see the knob turning, or perhaps even hear a gentle knock.

But instead, the whispering grew bolder, like a voice testing its strength. She could make out faint words now, though they were jumbled, strange phrases that sent a shiver through her:

"Forgotten... so long... alone... come... closer..."

She gripped the edge of her blanket, her fingers tense, every part of her urging her to stay still, to be silent, as if making a sound would invite whatever was outside to press closer. Her mind raced, piecing together fragments of memory, the warnings, the rules. Mrs. Havers' words came rushing back: There are movements in the night.

She wanted to call out, to demand who—or what—was outside her door, but her voice felt trapped, caught somewhere between fear and disbelief. After what felt like an eternity, the whispers softened, fading into a faint, unintelligible murmur that receded down the hall, followed by the tapping sounds that grew more and more distant.

The silence that returned was heavier than before, filled with a lingering presence that she could feel even after the sounds had vanished. It was as though the air itself had shifted, thickened, the walls holding onto the memory of the whispers, the taps. She lay there, frozen, her mind racing, struggling to make sense of what had just happened. But the explanation eluded her, slipping through her thoughts like shadows in the dark.

She must have lain awake for hours, her ears attuned to every creak and shift in the house, but the whispers did not return, and neither did the tapping. Eventually, exhaustion took over, and Mara slipped into a fitful sleep, her dreams plagued by the sound of distant voices and footsteps just beyond her reach.

When morning finally broke, weak and pale through her window, she rose from bed with a strange, lingering dread, the memory of the night still fresh in her mind. She wanted to shake it off, to tell herself it had all been her imagination, a figment of an overactive mind stirred by the manor's strange atmosphere. But the memories lingered, clinging to her like cobwebs.

Downstairs, Mrs. Havers was already preparing breakfast, moving around the kitchen with her usual quiet efficiency. Mara watched her, wondering if she should say something, if she should ask about the strange noises. But she hesitated, unsure how to phrase her experience without sounding foolish.

Instead, she settled into a seat at the table, her mind still wrestling with the events of the night. After a few moments, she gathered her courage and cleared her throat.

"Mrs. Havers," she began cautiously, "do you... ever hear strange sounds in the house? At night?"

Mrs. Havers' hands stilled for the briefest moment before she continued setting out the tea, her expression carefully neutral. "Old houses make sounds," she said, her tone calm but with an edge of finality. "Especially a place as old as Blackwood Manor."

Mara felt a slight frustration prickling at her. She leaned forward, trying to convey the seriousness of her question. "I know houses creak, but... these weren't ordinary sounds. I heard whispering. Tapping. It was as if someone was... outside my door."

Mrs. Havers looked up, her gaze sharp, a hint of something—concern, perhaps?—flashing in her eyes. But she quickly masked it, her face smoothing back into its usual composure.

"As I said," Mrs. Havers replied slowly, "Blackwood Manor is an old house. It has its... peculiarities." She paused, her gaze hardening. "That is why we keep our doors locked at night, Miss Fenton."

Her words settled over Mara like a warning, a reminder that the rules were not simply suggestions but boundaries meant to keep something at bay. The frustration in Mara's chest ebbed, replaced by a cold, sinking realization: whatever she had heard, Mrs. Havers was not surprised. In fact, it seemed she expected it.

Mara nodded slowly, her gaze drifting down to her untouched cup of tea. She didn't press further, sensing that Mrs. Havers would not reveal more, not yet. But a seed of fear had taken root, its tendrils winding through her mind. She had followed the house rules, yet the sounds had come to her door anyway, as if testing her resolve, or perhaps inviting her to come closer, to break the boundaries that Mrs. Havers had set so carefully.

As she sat in the dim morning light, Mara wondered what would happen if she did cross those boundaries—if she ignored the house's rules, stepped into the east wing, or ascended to the forbidden attic. The thought made her shiver, but it also stirred something else in her—a strange, reckless curiosity, a need to understand the house's secrets.

But for now, she would heed the rules. She would lock her door at night, keep her questions quiet, and hope that whatever had wandered the halls last night would not come calling again. Yet deep down, she knew that this would not be the last time she'd hear the whispers, that the house had barely begun to reveal itself.

And in the depths of her mind, she could still hear the faint tapping, the whispering that called to her in words she could not understand, beckoning her closer to the heart of Blackwood Manor.

Chapter 6: A Discovery in the Library

The days at Blackwood Manor had taken on a peculiar rhythm. By day, the house felt almost tranquil, shrouded in the muted light of winter, its vast rooms still and quiet. But by night, Mara found herself holding her breath, locking her door with a firm, deliberate hand and lying awake, her senses straining for any sound that might betray the house's secrets. She had come to accept the rules—though not without suspicion—and each night since the tapping and whispers, she'd locked her door without question, hoping it would be enough.

But her curiosity about the house only deepened. What lay hidden in the east wing? What kind of relics were stored in the attic? And why did she sense that the house was watching her, assessing her like a guest it might not be ready to welcome?

One afternoon, unable to resist the urge for answers, Mara made her way to the library. It was one of the few rooms in the house that felt almost welcoming, with dark shelves stretching from floor to ceiling, each one stuffed with books that looked as old as the manor itself. A large, ornate desk sat by the window, casting shadows across the thick carpet, and the air smelled faintly of leather and dust—a strangely comforting scent amidst the vast coldness of the manor.

Mara began scanning the shelves, her fingers brushing over titles that ranged from ancient history to occult studies, poetry to philosophy. She pulled down a few volumes here and there, hoping to find something, anything, that might tell her more about Blackwood Manor and the mysterious woman who had bequeathed it to her.

After nearly an hour of fruitless searching, she noticed a small, leather-bound book nestled between two larger tomes on the lowest shelf. The spine was worn, the leather cracked, as though it had been handled often and with great care. She pulled it out, her fingers brushing over the embossed initials on the cover: S.B.

Her pulse quickened as she flipped it open, her eyes skimming the faded ink on the yellowed pages. It was a journal, and from the first few lines, she knew exactly whose it was—Seraphina Blackwood, the widow herself.

She felt a surge of excitement, mixed with apprehension, as she began to read the first entry, written in a neat, precise hand:

August 5th, 1893

It has been three years since Henry's passing, and still, I feel his absence like a knife pressed against my skin. The manor feels hollow without him, each room a cold reminder of what I have lost. They tell me I must let go, that grief will pass like a storm. But they are wrong. It festers, growing thicker with every day that I remain here, alone.

The words struck Mara with their rawness, a grief so deep it seemed to bleed from the page. She could almost picture the widow in the long, empty halls, dressed in black, her eyes shadowed with sorrow. The entries continued, chronicling a descent into isolation and obsession. Each entry seemed darker than the last, her tone growing more desperate as her grief turned inward, consuming her.

September 14th, 1893

They come to me in dreams—those who have gone before, voices I can no longer distinguish. I see Henry in the shadows, just out of reach, beckoning me to follow. I have begun to study the old ways, the ancient rites. If death is a barrier, then perhaps I may find a way to break through. I will bring him back to me.

Mara felt her hands tremble as she read. The widow had been consumed not only by grief but by a fixation on piercing the boundary between life and death. She had turned to arcane practices, forbidden rituals that hinted at dark things lurking just beyond the veil. The journal detailed her experiments, her attempts to reach her husband in whatever realm he had passed into. She'd consulted books on necromancy, studied ancient symbols, and even conducted midnight rituals in an attempt to commune with him.

The desperation in her words was palpable, growing with each entry until it became an all-consuming obsession.

November 2nd, 1893

The house has changed. I feel it responding to me, as if it too desires what I seek. Last night, the wind howled through the east wing, and I swear I saw him—just a flicker, a shadow cast against the wall. Henry. I am so close. This place is my ally now; it understands what I need. I feel his presence, tethered to the stones and wood of this manor. Soon, he will return to me.

Mara shivered, feeling as though the widow's words were casting a spell over her, binding her into the strange, tragic tale that had unfolded within these walls. It was clear that Seraphina had not merely mourned her husband's death; she had let it consume her entirely, twisting her love into something dark and unnatural. She had turned Blackwood Manor into a vessel for her longing, an anchor for the spirit she so desperately sought to bring back.

Then, one entry in particular caught Mara's eye. The words were scrawled in a hasty, almost frantic script, as though Seraphina had written them in the grip of some overpowering emotion.

December 3rd, 1893

I have succeeded, but it is not as I expected. He is here—oh, he is here—but he is not what he was. I see shadows in his eyes, things I did not understand before. The house... it has taken something from him, and now he lingers, not as my Henry, but as something else, something bound. I fear I have gone too far. This place has a hunger of its own, a need that feeds on my sorrow, on his spirit. I wanted him back, but I have trapped us both in this place, and now... I fear there is no escape.

The entry ended abruptly, the ink smudged as though she had closed the journal in haste. Mara felt a chill seep into her bones as she read, realizing that Seraphina's obsession had not brought her husband back to her as she had hoped. Instead, it seemed to have twisted him, binding him to the manor in some unnatural state, a shadow of his former self. And the house—it was clear that Blackwood Manor itself had somehow responded, feeding off her grief and longing, becoming more than just a passive structure. It had transformed into a kind of prison, a web that held them both within its walls.

Mara closed the journal slowly, her hands trembling as she clutched it to her chest. She felt as though the widow's spirit lingered in the room, watching her reaction, perhaps waiting to see if Mara would make the same mistakes. The journal painted a portrait of a woman who had loved too deeply, so much that it had unmade her, trapping her in a cycle of longing and despair that transcended death.

As Mara sat in the dim light of the library, the weight of the house seemed to press down on her, thick with sorrow and secrets. Blackwood Manor wasn't just a home; it was a monument to Seraphina's grief, a labyrinth of longing and madness. And Mara, the distant relative summoned to inherit it, was now entwined in its dark legacy.

But more than that, she understood that Seraphina's influence hadn't faded with her death. The house had become something more—an entity shaped by her anguish, by her relentless pursuit of the impossible. And now, that entity seemed aware of Mara, watching her, testing her, as though wondering if she too would succumb to its pull.

Mara carefully slid the journal back onto the shelf, her mind spinning with questions. She didn't know what exactly lay within Blackwood Manor, what echoes of Seraphina's rituals lingered in its walls. But she knew one thing with a certainty that made her heart pound: the house was alive in its own way, and it would demand something from her in time.

As she turned to leave the library, a whisper seemed to drift through the air—a faint, ghostly sigh that stirred the dust in the dim light. Mara froze, her skin prickling, and for a moment she thought she heard the faintest trace of Seraphina's voice, as though the widow's spirit lingered, bound within the house she had transformed.

"Closer... come closer..."

The words were almost inaudible, barely more than a breath, but Mara felt them settle over her, curling around her heart like a silent promise. She left the library quickly, her pulse racing, the memory of the widow's journal haunting her steps.

She knew now that the house held far more than she had bargained for. And as she returned to her room, Mara couldn't shake the feeling that she had already begun to walk a path Seraphina had paved long ago—a path that would lead her deeper into the shadows of Blackwood Manor.

Chapter 7: The Creaking Floorboards

The night descended over Blackwood Manor with an almost unnatural stillness, the air thick and stagnant, as if the house itself were holding its breath. Mara locked her door as she had every night since arriving, checking the bolt twice, her mind still buzzing with the revelations from Seraphina's journal. She tried to settle herself, but the widow's words lingered, weaving through her thoughts like threads in a dark tapestry. The journal had left her with questions she couldn't answer—questions about the nature of the house, about the forces that seemed to reside within it, and most unsettlingly, about her own place in its twisted legacy.

The manor was quiet as she climbed into bed, pulling the blankets up to her chin and listening to the silence pressing against her door. The room was pitch black save for a faint sliver of moonlight that cut through the heavy curtains. Her ears strained, searching for any hint of sound, a familiar tension building in her chest. Since that first night, she had heard little more than the house's usual creaks and groans, but tonight, something felt different.

Then, she heard it.

A soft, deliberate creak, the unmistakable sound of weight pressing down on an old floorboard, somewhere down the hall. Her breath hitched as she lay still, listening intently, her heart beginning to race. The sound came again, louder this time, followed by another, each step slow and deliberate, echoing through the empty corridors.

It was as if someone were pacing, their movements steady, unhurried, almost methodical.

Mara's mind raced. Perhaps it was Mrs. Havers, checking the house as she did at night, making sure everything was secure. But something in the rhythm of the footsteps unsettled her; they were too slow, too heavy. They didn't match the careful, quiet way Mrs. Havers moved.

These footsteps felt different—alien, even—as if they belonged to someone or something with a different purpose altogether.

The creaking grew louder, and Mara's breath came faster as the footsteps drew nearer, moving closer and closer to her door. She squeezed her eyes shut, gripping the edges of the blanket, every muscle tense. She tried to convince herself it was just the house, an old structure settling under its own weight, or a draft pushing a door somewhere down the hall. But the sounds didn't stop; they persisted, steady and relentless.

The footsteps paused, just outside her room.

A shiver of terror ran through her, and her skin prickled as if she could feel the presence standing there, just beyond the door. She held her breath, afraid that even the smallest sound would give her away, as if whatever was outside would sense her fear, would push open the door and step inside. Her gaze locked on the door, watching for any sign of movement, any hint of a shadow passing under the crack of light at the threshold.

After what felt like an eternity, the footsteps resumed, their sound muffled now as they moved away from her door and down the hall. Mara let out a shaky breath, her chest tight with fear, her heart pounding so loudly she was sure it echoed through the room. She listened, hearing the footsteps grow softer, more distant, until finally, the silence returned, deep and absolute.

But Mara didn't move. She lay there, her eyes fixed on the door, her ears straining for any hint that the footsteps might come back. The house was still, but she felt its weight pressing down on her, as if it were aware of her fear, savouring it. Minutes passed, but sleep refused to come, her mind replaying the slow, deliberate creaks of the floorboards, each step etched into her memory.

The footsteps returned the next night.

This time, Mara was wide awake, waiting for them, her body tense with anticipation. They started just after midnight, the same slow, deliberate steps echoing through the halls, drawing closer with every passing second. She lay in bed, her muscles taut, trying to convince herself that it was all in her mind, that perhaps she was just imagining things. But the footsteps were unmistakable, growing louder as they approached her room, just as they had the night before.

Again, they paused outside her door, and Mara felt a chill seep through her as she listened, her breath shallow, her heart racing. She could almost feel a presence on the other side, waiting, listening, as if aware of her fear, feeding off it. Her hand drifted toward the bedside table, where she had placed the journal, as though touching it might somehow protect her.

She stayed like that, motionless, until the footsteps finally moved on, fading down the hall and leaving her alone in the heavy silence.

By the third night, Mara was exhausted, her nerves frayed, her mind filled with fragments of Seraphina's journal, the whispered warnings, the tapping and footsteps that haunted her in the dark. She couldn't ignore the sensation that something was happening, that the house was trying to tell her something, or perhaps lure her into something she could not yet understand.

Desperation overcame her, and she decided that she couldn't lie there passively, waiting for the footsteps to come again. She needed answers. She needed to know if it was Mrs. Havers, or if something else—something connected to Seraphina's rituals, her obsessions—was walking the halls at night.

She rose quietly, her movements careful as she slipped out of bed, pulling a heavy shawl around her shoulders for warmth. She approached the door, her heart pounding, and placed her ear against the wood, listening to the silence beyond. The hallway was empty, but the weight of the house seemed to press against her, a silent, watchful presence lurking in the darkness.

Mara unlocked the door slowly, wincing at the faint click as she turned the key. She pushed it open a fraction, peering into the hallway.

The dim light from the wall sconces cast long shadows along the corridor, and the air felt colder than usual, as if the warmth had been sucked from the space.

Taking a deep breath, she stepped into the hall, her bare feet silent against the floor. She walked slowly, her gaze darting back and forth, half-expecting to see a shadow move or hear the footsteps resume. The hall was empty, but the sense of being watched was palpable, a prickling sensation that made her skin crawl.

She followed the corridor toward the main staircase, feeling an inexplicable pull, a compulsion to go deeper into the house, to seek out the source of the footsteps that had haunted her nights. But as she reached the landing, she heard it—a faint creak, somewhere in the shadows behind her.

Mara froze, her breath catching in her throat. The sound was unmistakable—the slow, heavy creak of a floorboard, as though someone were right behind her, watching her every move. She turned, but the hallway was empty, its shadows stretching out in eerie silence.

Then, she heard a whisper.

"Come... closer..."

The words sent a jolt through her, chilling her to the core. She spun around, searching the shadows, but there was no one there. The hallway was empty, silent, the house seeming to hold its breath as it waited for her next move. The whisper echoed in her mind, a call that stirred something dark and restless within her.

And then, just as suddenly, the footsteps began again, moving slowly toward her from down the hall. Mara backed away, her heart pounding, her hands clenched at her sides. The presence felt closer than ever, almost tangible, as though the house itself were reaching out to her, drawing her deeper into its web.

In a surge of fear, she turned and fled back to her room, her footsteps silent and swift as she locked the door behind her. She leaned against it, gasping for breath, her mind racing with questions and the memory of that whisper echoing through her thoughts.

Come... closer.

She sank onto the edge of the bed, pressing her hands to her face, her mind swirling with fragments of the widow's journal, the footsteps, the whispered warnings. Whatever lingered in the house, it wanted her attention, drawing her closer with each passing night, unravelling her resolve one footstep at a time.

As she lay back in bed, her eyes fixed on the ceiling, she felt the weight of Blackwood Manor settle over her once more. The house was alive, pulsing with secrets, and she was caught within it, a stranger drawn into a web of grief, obsession, and something darker still.

And she knew, with a strange, undeniable certainty, that the footsteps would return again.

Chapter 8: The Widow's Room

For days, Mara had managed to resist the call of the east wing. Mrs. Havers' warnings replayed in her mind whenever she passed the hallway that led to the forbidden part of the house, a reminder of the rules she'd promised to obey. Yet, each night, as the footsteps drew closer and the whispers grew bolder, a reckless curiosity bloomed in her, mingling with a sense of inevitability.

The house was pressing her, testing her, whispering secrets that begged to be heard. And after another sleepless night haunted by whispers, Mara could no longer resist.

In the dim light of early morning, when Blackwood Manor seemed almost peaceful, she made her way to the east wing. She moved slowly, her heart pounding with a mixture of fear and anticipation. The corridor was colder here, its walls lined with portraits that seemed older than the rest of the house. Their eyes watched her as she walked, filled with an unsettling awareness, as if they, too, were judging her choice to break the house's most solemn rule.

Finally, she reached a door at the end of the corridor, a grand, arched entryway with a faded brass handle that gleamed dully in the grey light. She hesitated, her hand hovering over the handle, a last remnant of caution flaring within her. But something in the air, a heavy, expectant silence, seemed to pull her forward. Taking a deep breath, she turned the handle and pushed the door open.

The room beyond was cloaked in shadows, the curtains drawn tightly across the windows, casting the space in an eerie half-light. As her eyes adjusted, Mara took in the details, her pulse quickening as the atmosphere seemed to shift around her, the air thick with something ancient and unsettling.

The room was vast, its walls lined with furniture shrouded in sheets that sagged under the weight of dust and cobwebs. The shapes beneath the sheets hinted at lavish armchairs, a vanity, perhaps even a wardrobe, all frozen in time. The room felt as though it had been untouched for decades, as if it were waiting for someone to return and breathe life into its decaying elegance.

In the center of the room was a large four-poster bed, draped in thick, blackened curtains that hung like a veil of mourning. Mara approached it slowly, her gaze drawn to the shape of the bed beneath the shroud, a strange dread pooling in her stomach. The fabric was woven with intricate patterns of flowers and vines, faded but beautiful, as if even death could not strip the room of its once-grand beauty.

But what caught her attention most was the vanity across from the bed, its mirror clouded and dull. A thin layer of dust coated the surface, but Mara could still make out faint traces of fingerprints across the glass, as if someone had touched it recently, disturbing the dust.

On the vanity sat a small collection of personal effects: an old hairbrush, its bristles worn, a delicate hand mirror with a cracked handle, a vial of perfume long evaporated but still faintly fragrant. And draped across the vanity stool, as if waiting to be worn, was a black veil, its fabric sheer and dark, like a shadow spun into cloth.

Mara reached out, her fingers trembling as they brushed against the veil. The fabric was softer than she expected, almost silk-like, and as she held it up, she imagined Seraphina Blackwood sitting at this very vanity, draping the veil over her hair, her gaze distant as she prepared herself for a life of mourning.

But as Mara held the veil, she felt an inexplicable urge—a compulsion that seemed to come from outside herself. She glanced into the mirror, her reflection barely visible through the dust, and, almost without thinking, she lifted the veil and placed it over her own head.

The effect was immediate. The room around her seemed to shift, growing darker, the shadows stretching across the floor like reaching hands. The air grew colder, pressing against her skin like icy fingers, and a faint sound began to fill her ears—a whispering, like voices caught in the wind, soft and mournful.

Her heartbeat quickened as she stared at her reflection in the mirror, her face obscured by the veil, her features blending with the shadows. She could almost see someone else in the mirror—a woman with haunted eyes, her expression one of sorrow and defiance. Mara's own face seemed to blur, to fade, until she felt as though she were looking into the eyes of Seraphina herself.

A sudden flood of emotion surged through her—grief, longing, an overwhelming sense of loss. It was as if the veil had opened a door, connecting her to the widow's memories, to the pain that had saturated these walls. For a moment, Mara felt trapped in another life, caught in the depths of an all-consuming sorrow that was not her own.

And then, just as quickly, the spell broke. She tore the veil from her head, gasping for breath, the room snapping back into its dim reality. She felt disoriented, as if she had just woken from a vivid dream, her heart racing, her skin prickling with the remnants of whatever presence had seeped into her mind.

Her gaze drifted back to the bed, and she noticed something she hadn't seen before—a small leather-bound book resting on the bedside table, half-hidden beneath the dust. Mara crossed the room and picked it up, her fingers brushing away the dirt to reveal the initials "S.B." embossed on the cover. Another journal.

She hesitated, feeling the weight of the book in her hands, a strange reluctance washing over her. But curiosity won out, and she opened the journal, flipping to a random page. The handwriting was hurried, the ink smudged, as though Seraphina had written it in haste:

"I hear him at night, pacing the halls. The house has him, holds him. I see him in the mirrors, in the corners of the room, watching me. But he is not what he was. He is... changed. I have bound him here, and now he lingers, half-formed, trapped in the shadow of what he once was."

Mara felt a shiver run through her as she read. The journal entry continued, describing how Seraphina had bound her husband's spirit to the manor, attempting to bring him back from death. But something had gone wrong. Whatever she had summoned was not her husband, but a twisted echo, a spirit caught between realms, lingering in the house, bound to its walls and floors.

The entry ended abruptly, the last lines smudged, as though Seraphina had been interrupted. Mara closed the journal, her mind reeling, the room around her seeming darker, more oppressive.

She placed the journal back on the table and turned to leave, but as she moved, she felt a strange resistance, as if the room itself were reluctant to let her go. The air seemed to thicken, pressing against her, and she heard the faintest sound—a whisper, a voice too soft to discern but filled with an unmistakable sadness.

She glanced back at the veil, draped once more over the vanity, and felt a pang of sympathy for Seraphina, a woman who had loved too fiercely, who had attempted to defy death itself, only to trap herself in a prison of her own making.

Mara moved quickly, leaving the room and closing the door behind her, the weight of the widow's sorrow following her down the hall. She felt drained, as if the house had taken something from her, leaving her with a hollow ache in her chest.

As she made her way back to the west wing, Mara couldn't shake the feeling that she had crossed a boundary, that by entering the widow's room, she had awoken something dormant, a presence that now watched her with renewed interest.

And as she closed her own door and locked it, her hands trembling, she knew that Blackwood Manor was not finished with her. She had glimpsed the shadows of its past, felt the pull of its secrets, and there was no turning back. The house had drawn her deeper into its web, and Mara could only wonder what other secrets lay waiting in the darkened halls, whispering her name, beckoning her closer.

Chapter 9: The Neighbour's Warning

After the encounter in the widow's room, Mara couldn't shake the feeling of unease that clung to her. She felt watched, as though invisible eyes followed her through the halls, their presence pressing down on her whenever she let her guard down. Nights were worse now; the footsteps outside her door had resumed, more persistent than before, their rhythm slower, more deliberate, like someone testing the patience of her locked door.

By day, Blackwood Manor was hauntingly quiet, as if recovering from its nighttime vigilance. After a few days of restlessness, Mara decided she needed a break from the house, a chance to breathe fresh air and perhaps shake off the oppressive feeling that had settled over her like a dark cloud. She ventured into the nearby village—a small, sleepy place with winding streets, quaint cottages, and locals who eyed her with a mixture of curiosity and, she noted with some discomfort, thinly veiled caution.

It wasn't long before she found a small café, tucked into the corner of the village square, with a simple sign that read Elder's Brew. Inside, a handful of patrons sat nursing warm drinks, and Mara could feel the atmosphere shift as she entered. The murmurs quieted, and a few heads turned, eyes narrowing as they took her in. She felt an unsettling familiarity with their gazes, as though she were being studied, much like the house had studied her.

She ordered a tea and took a seat by the window, allowing herself to relax as she gazed out over the square. Just as she settled into her drink, an older man seated at a nearby table cleared his throat, catching her attention.

"You're staying up at Blackwood Manor, aren't you?" he asked, his voice low but with a hint of interest.

Mara looked up, surprised by the question but nodding cautiously. "Yes, I am. How did you know?"

The man chuckled softly, a knowing gleam in his eye. "This village is small, miss. News of anyone at that manor spreads fast." He took a long sip of his coffee, studying her over the rim of his cup. "Can't say we expected to see anyone new up there, not after all that's happened."

A ripple of unease passed through her. "What do you mean?"

The man set his cup down and leaned in slightly, his voice dropping to a near-whisper. "Blackwood Manor's got a dark history, miss. Goes back generations. Strange things have always happened up there. People say it's cursed. Haunted, even."

The word "haunted" echoed in her mind, bringing back memories of the footsteps, the whispers, the veil in the widow's room. She forced herself to stay calm, curious to hear more. "Haunted? By who?"

"By who?" The man gave a mirthless chuckle, shaking his head. "By the house itself, some say. And by Seraphina Blackwood, that widow who lived up there until she passed. She was... different. Strange, even when she was alive. Kept to herself, always talking of spirits and the like, a woman obsessed with the dead." He paused, his expression darkening. "But it was worse after her husband died. They say she went mad with grief, started dabbling in things best left alone. There were rumours—talk of strange ceremonies, visitors to the house who came and left in the dead of night."

Mara felt a chill as the man spoke. It was as though he were describing the very things she had glimpsed in Seraphina's journal—the widow's desperation, her obsession with the supernatural, her attempts to bridge the gap between life and death. The man continued, his tone growing sombre.

"She was seen less and less in her final years, until she vanished altogether. No one knows how she died or what happened to her. All we know is that the house changed after she passed. People who stayed there reported hearing voices, seeing figures in the mirrors, and... worse."

Mara's stomach twisted. "Worse?"

The man hesitated, his gaze flickering to the other villagers seated nearby, as if gauging whether they would listen in. Leaning closer, he dropped his voice to a near-whisper. "Several people have tried to stay at Blackwood Manor over the years. Relatives, caretakers... even a few treasure-seekers hoping to find some relics of the Blackwood's' wealth. But they all left, or... disappeared." He looked her squarely in the eye. "The ones who came back were never the same. They spoke of shadows in the halls, of dreams that felt too real, like something was pulling them deeper and deeper into the house."

He paused, as though carefully weighing his next words. "One of them—the last caretaker who stayed there—he told me he felt as if he were being watched at all times, as if the walls themselves were listening, waiting for him to break. Said he heard footsteps at night, tapping on his door, and voices calling his name."

Mara's heart pounded as the man's words mirrored her own experiences in the manor. She took a shaky breath, steeling herself. "Did he... did he say what the voices wanted?"

The man nodded, his expression grim. "They wanted him to stay. To join them, he said." He paused, lowering his voice even further. "Some say the house has a hunger to it, that it binds people to it, trapping them in its walls. They think Seraphina did something to that house, left a part of herself there that won't let go. She spent so many years trying to call her husband back from the dead... that perhaps she bound herself to the house instead."

Mara felt a cold sweat break out over her skin, her heart pounding as memories of her nights in the manor came flooding back. The footsteps outside her door, the whispering voice calling her closer, the weight of the house pressing in on her. She tried to steady herself, though her hands trembled slightly. "So... what happened to those people who left?"

The man's gaze grew distant, his face drawn with a strange sadness. "They lived, but they were hollow, empty, as if they'd left a part of themselves behind in that place. Some of them wouldn't speak about what they'd seen. Others... well, they just couldn't stop talking, almost as if they'd lost touch with reality. They'd repeat the same things, over and over, like they were stuck in a loop." He met her gaze, his eyes serious. "If I were you, miss, I'd get out of there while you still can. Leave that place behind and don't look back."

Mara felt a prickle of fear mixed with an odd sense of defiance. The house had a strange hold on her, one she didn't fully understand, but she couldn't simply abandon it. There was a legacy there, a story that needed to be uncovered, and part of her felt almost drawn to it, as though Seraphina herself were urging her on.

"Thank you for the warning," she said, her voice steady despite the tension in her chest. "But I need to understand what happened there. There's something about the house... something I can't explain, but I have to see it through."

The man sighed, giving her a weary look. "Curiosity can be a dangerous thing, miss. Blackwood Manor... it's a place that draws you in, but it doesn't always let you go. It's a web, and Seraphina spun it herself. People like you—those who feel that pull—you're the ones it wants. You might think you're in control, but that house has a way of taking what it wants, whether you're willing or not."

Mara felt his words sink into her, a warning that resonated with an unsettling truth. But the pull of Blackwood Manor was undeniable. It was as if the house had chosen her, calling her to piece together its mysteries, to understand the dark history that pulsed within its walls.

She finished her tea in silence, her mind racing as she replayed the man's words. As she left the café, the villagers' gazes followed her, a silent judgment in their eyes. She felt a strange sense of isolation, as though she had crossed a boundary simply by returning to the house, setting herself apart from those who understood its dangers and had chosen to keep their distance.

The walk back to Blackwood Manor felt longer than before, the shadows growing deeper as the sun dipped behind thick clouds. When she reached the front gate, she paused, glancing back toward the village, a lingering doubt gnawing at her. The house stood before her, silent and dark, its windows like empty eyes watching her approach.

But even as she hesitated, the feeling returned—that pull, the silent urging that seemed to emanate from the walls themselves. She took a deep breath and stepped through the gates, her footsteps carrying her back into the shadows of Blackwood Manor.

The warning echoed in her mind, a whispered caution that mingled with the house's quiet call:

"It's a web... and you're the one it wants."

As she entered the house, closing the heavy door behind her, Mara felt the familiar chill of the manor settle over her once more, a silent, watchful presence that welcomed her home.

Part II: The Widow's Shadow
Chapter 10: The Locked Door

Mara awoke to a pale, cold light filtering through her curtains, casting the room in a faint glow. Her mind felt foggy, heavy with fragments of the previous day's conversations—the villager's warning, his insistence that Blackwood Manor was a web, waiting to ensnare those who came too close. She had slept fitfully, her dreams haunted by images of shadows moving through empty halls, voices calling her name, urging her deeper into the heart of the house.

After dressing, she made her way downstairs, intending to seek some comfort in the quiet of the morning. She moved through the familiar hallways, the silence punctuated only by the soft creaks and whispers of the old manor. But as she rounded the corner toward the library, she stopped short, her gaze landing on something that sent a chill through her.

A door that had always been locked—one she had tugged on countless times out of curiosity—now stood slightly ajar.

Mara stared at it, a mix of curiosity and trepidation swirling within her. She had passed this door daily, wondering what lay beyond it, but had always respected the barrier. There was no reason for it to be open; Mrs. Havers had told her plainly that certain parts of the house were best left alone, locked and untouched. Yet here it was, slightly open, almost as if it were inviting her in.

She took a hesitant step forward, her pulse quickening. The air around the door felt colder, an invisible threshold that seemed to separate this room from the rest of the manor. She placed her hand on the door, feeling the chill of the wood seep into her palm, and pushed it open.

Inside, the room was dim, lit only by the faint, filtered light that seeped through heavily draped windows. Dust hung in the air, swirling in the faint rays, and the silence here felt different, thicker, as if it had been undisturbed for years. She stepped inside, her gaze drifting over the untouched furniture, the faint outline of a bed beneath a heavy canopy, and a writing desk cluttered with trinkets and items that seemed frozen in time.

A strange sense of familiarity washed over her, though she couldn't remember ever seeing this room. It felt like stepping into a memory, or perhaps even a dream—a place suspended between past and present.

She moved slowly, her fingers trailing over the delicate lace of the bed canopy, the cool surface of an old perfume bottle left on the nightstand. Everything was coated in a fine layer of dust, as if the room had been waiting, untouched, for someone to return. The faint scent of lavender lingered in the air, a ghost of a fragrance that might have once filled the room.

Mara's gaze fell on the walls, which were lined with framed photographs and faded portraits. She stepped closer, her heart catching in her throat as she realized who she was looking at—Seraphina Blackwood. The woman in the photographs looked younger than the haunting portrait she had seen in the hallway, her gaze softer, her expression less burdened. In one image, Seraphina stood with a man who must have been her husband, his hand resting on her shoulder, his face warm and gentle.

She felt a pang of sadness as she took in the couple's likeness, the happiness that seemed to linger in their faces, forever captured in these old photographs. Seraphina had once been a woman in love, a woman with hopes and dreams—a stark contrast to the grieving widow who had descended into obsession and despair.

At the far end of the room, something caught her eye: a small, ornate chest resting atop a table, its surface engraved with intricate floral patterns. Unlike the other items in the room, this chest looked pristine, as though it had been polished recently. Curiosity overpowered her caution as she reached out, running her fingers along the cool metal.

With a slight hesitation, she opened the chest, her hands trembling as she lifted the lid. Inside lay a collection of letters, bound with a frayed ribbon, their edges yellowed with age. Mara picked up the first letter, unfolding it carefully, and her eyes skimmed over the elegant script.

My dearest Seraphina,

The days are long without you by my side. I count the moments until we are together again, until I can hold you and whisper to you the words I can never seem to express on paper. Please, my love, stay well, and know that my heart is with you, always.

The letter was signed Henry. Mara felt a lump in her throat as she read the words, as though she were glimpsing a love story hidden within these walls, a story that had been swallowed by time and tragedy. She read several more letters, each one more heartfelt than the last, the words filled with promises, endearments, plans for a future that had never come to pass.

A soft creak echoed through the room, breaking her concentration. Mara froze, her heart pounding as she looked up, half-expecting to see someone standing in the doorway. But the room was empty, silent save for the faint rustling of the dust particles suspended in the air.

Still clutching the letters, she turned toward the writing desk, where an old, leather-bound journal lay, its cover worn and cracked. The initials "S.B." were embossed in faded gold lettering on the cover. Her pulse quickened as she reached for the journal, sensing that this might hold answers, perhaps even explanations.

She flipped it open, skimming the pages, her eyes drawn to Seraphina's words.

"The nights grow colder. I feel him here, though I know it is only a shadow of what once was. I light the candles, I perform the rites, but he does not come. Perhaps I was wrong, perhaps I asked too much. But my heart will not let go. I will not let go."

Mara shivered as she read, the despair in the words like a weight pressing down on her chest. The entries grew darker, more frantic, as Seraphina described her attempts to call her husband's spirit back, to bind him to the house, so that he would never truly leave her. But her efforts had only left her feeling emptier, each ritual widening the distance between them instead of bridging it.

She could almost feel Seraphina's presence in the room, a spectral sadness that filled the space, thickening the air until Mara found it difficult to breathe. Her eyes drifted to the final entry, written in a shaky hand, the words barely legible.

"It is done. The house is his prison, and mine. I have bound us both to this place, for better or worse. But the shadows grow darker. They move on their own. Sometimes, I feel them watching me. I hear whispers in the night, footsteps in the hall. They say I have taken something that was not mine to take, that there will be a price. But I cannot undo what I have done. I can only endure, for now, and hope..."

The last word trailed off, the ink smudged as though Seraphina's hand had trembled, or perhaps something had interrupted her. Mara closed the journal slowly, a chill settling over her. The room felt different now, heavier, as though it held the weight of Seraphina's final act, her last desperate attempt to reclaim what she had lost.

She placed the letters and the journal back in the chest, closing it with trembling hands. As she stood, a soft sound caught her attention—a faint whisper, like a breath of wind brushing against her ear. Her skin prickled, and she turned slowly, half-expecting to see a figure in the corner, or perhaps a flicker of movement in the shadows.

But the room was empty.

She took a step back, her heart pounding, a sense of dread growing within her. She turned to leave, and as she reached the doorway, she glanced back at the room, the bed shrouded in dust, the photographs on the wall, the letters tucked away, all relics of a life consumed by love and loss.

She closed the door softly behind her, leaving the room in its ghostly stillness, and locked it, feeling the weight of her discovery settle over her like a veil.

As she made her way back down the hall, the realization struck her with a chilling certainty: Seraphina had bound herself to the house, but she had bound more than herself—she had bound Henry, too, or whatever shadowed remnant remained of him, and now they both lingered, locked in a place neither could leave.

The house wasn't just haunted by its memories; it was a prison, a web spun by grief and obsession, one that now held Mara in its grip as well.

And deep down, she knew that whatever had drawn her to this room, to this locked door, was far from finished with her.

Chapter 11: Dreams of the Past

The first dream came that night, slipping into Mara's mind as she finally drifted into an uneasy sleep. It started subtly, like a whisper at the edge of consciousness, but soon it grew vivid, all-consuming, pulling her into a reality that felt tangible, almost too real.

In the dream, she was standing in Blackwood Manor, but it was different. The walls were brighter, the furniture pristine, the air filled with the faint scent of lavender and candle wax. She was wearing a long, dark dress that swished against the wooden floors as she moved. She looked down, seeing her hands—hands that were not her own, thin and pale, the fingers adorned with rings that glinted in the flickering candlelight.

She knew, instinctively, that she was Seraphina.

Mara felt her heart race as she moved through the halls, her footsteps echoing softly. She was drawn toward the east wing, her mind caught in a fog of grief and desperation, emotions that clung to her like a second skin. She could feel Seraphina's sorrow, her longing, a deep ache that seemed to burn within her.

The dream shifted, and she was standing in a candlelit room, surrounded by strange symbols etched into the floor. Her fingers traced the outline of a silver locket around her neck, and as she opened it, she saw a tiny portrait of a man inside—Henry. She felt Seraphina's longing surge, the overwhelming sense of loss pressing down on her chest like a weight.

In the dream, she was chanting softly, her voice carrying an ancient incantation, words Mara didn't understand yet somehow knew were powerful. She watched as Seraphina's hands moved with practiced precision, setting out objects—candles, flowers, a lock of hair, and a vial filled with a dark liquid. Each item held a meaning, a purpose, each one intended to call back the man she had loved and lost.

The air grew thick, almost alive, pulsing with an energy that felt dark and oppressive. Shadows flickered around her, stretching across the walls, twisting into strange shapes. She could feel a presence building, pressing in, as if the very walls were watching, waiting. But even as the ritual reached its peak, there was no sign of Henry. Only a sense of emptiness, of silence.

A whisper echoed in her mind: He's gone, he's gone, he's gone.

The dream fractured, and Mara felt herself pulled through a blur of images, each one more disorienting than the last. She saw glimpses of Seraphina wandering the empty halls of Blackwood Manor, her hair dishevelled, her dress trailing along the floor, her eyes hollow and haunted. The days bled into nights, and the nights into days, each one filled with the same unyielding ache. Seraphina would pace, call his name, weep in the stillness, her desperation mounting with every unanswered plea.

And then, one night, Mara felt the shift. She could feel it as Seraphina had felt it—a flicker of movement in the corner of her eye, a shadow where there should be none. She turned, feeling her heart leap with hope, a spark of belief that her husband had finally returned to her.

But the figure that emerged from the shadows wasn't Henry. It was something else, something dark and twisted, a hollow echo of the man she had loved. It lingered in the shadows, its face obscured, its movements jerky, unnatural. Seraphina's heart twisted in horror, and Mara felt her own heart race as she watched, helpless, caught in the widow's memories.

Seraphina tried to speak, to reach out, but the figure melted into the darkness, leaving only the faintest whisper behind.

You wanted him back. Now he is here.

The dream shifted again, and Mara found herself in Seraphina's room, staring at the mirror on the vanity. Seraphina's reflection stared back at her, her face pale, her eyes wide and haunted. But as she watched, her reflection seemed to change, the shadows deepening around her eyes, her mouth twisting into a grimace of despair. The room around her grew darker, the air heavy with the scent of lavender mixed with something metallic, something bitter.

Mara tried to look away, but she was trapped, forced to watch as Seraphina's reflection began to blur, her face twisting into a mask of anguish, her mouth opening in a silent scream. And as Mara stared, the reflection reached out, as if trying to pull her into the mirror, into the depths of Seraphina's grief and madness.

She woke with a start, her heart pounding, her skin slick with cold sweat. She was back in her bed, in the familiar shadows of her room in Blackwood Manor. But the terror lingered, the memory of the dream vivid and raw, as though she had truly lived through Seraphina's grief, felt the darkness settle over her like a suffocating veil.

Her hands trembled as she sat up, the remnants of the dream clinging to her like cobwebs. She could still feel the weight of Seraphina's loss, the hopelessness that had seeped into her soul, the same hopelessness that had driven her to attempt the impossible. Mara's thoughts were tangled, a whirlwind of emotions and images she could barely process.

She spent the day in a haze, the dream haunting her thoughts, a lingering presence that seemed to taint everything around her. She tried to shake it off, tried to tell herself it was only a dream, a trick of the mind brought on by her recent discoveries. But deep down, she knew it was something more, something darker.

The following night, the dream came again, more vivid, more intense.

This time, she was in the attic. The room was filled with strange artifacts, each one carefully placed, each one holding a strange, sinister energy. She saw Seraphina's hands reaching out, touching each item, her fingers lingering on an old, worn photograph, a lock of hair, a dark vial filled with some viscous liquid. She whispered to herself, her words soft, desperate, a mixture of pleading and anger.

I will bring him back to me. I will not let him go.

Mara felt her body ache with the force of Seraphina's need, her desperation to break the veil between life and death, to hold on to something that had long since slipped away. In the dream, the air was thick with incense, the room filled with shadows that danced and flickered in the candlelight, each one seeming to move with a life of its own.

As Seraphina's ritual intensified, the shadows grew denser, pressing in from all sides, their forms twisting into shapes that resembled faces—faces that watched her with dark, hollow eyes. Mara felt the weight of their gaze, a silent judgment that bore down on her, filling her with a sense of dread.

And then, in a whisper that seemed to come from everywhere and nowhere, she heard the voices.

He is not yours to bring back. There is a price for what you seek.

Seraphina ignored them, her focus unwavering as she continued the ritual. But Mara could feel the presence in the room growing stronger, darker, as though the shadows themselves were feeding off her desperation, drawing power from her grief.

The dream faded into darkness, leaving her with the echo of the voices and the suffocating weight of Seraphina's sorrow.

When she woke, she felt drained, as if the dreams had taken something from her, leaving her hollow and exhausted. The manor felt heavier, its atmosphere dense with an energy that seemed to press down on her, wrapping around her like a shroud. She could no longer ignore the dreams, could no longer tell herself they were simply figments of her imagination.

Mara knew, with a growing certainty, that Blackwood Manor was trying to show her something, to pull her deeper into its tangled web of memories and secrets. Each night, the dreams grew stronger, pulling her further into Seraphina's life, her grief, her obsession. It was as if the house itself was urging her to understand, to feel the pain that had bound Seraphina to this place, and to know the price of her choices.

And as Mara prepared for yet another sleepless night, she felt the chilling realization settle over her: she was not merely dreaming about Seraphina. She was living her memories, reliving her pain, experiencing the very moments that had transformed her from a grieving widow into a ghost that lingered within the walls of Blackwood Manor.

The house was calling her, drawing her closer, one dream at a time. And Mara knew she was running out of time to resist its pull.

Chapter 12: The Letter of Regret

After several nights of haunting dreams that felt more like memories than fantasies, Mara was left exhausted and haunted by Seraphina's sorrow. The dreams filled her waking hours as well, fragments of Seraphina's past bleeding into her thoughts, each one carrying with it an ache of betrayal and bitterness that was hard to shake.

She was in the library again, searching through the house's forgotten relics, trying to make sense of the widow's tragic story. The library had become her refuge, its heavy silence and dark shelves a balm against the oppressive weight of the manor. She scanned the shelves, hoping to uncover more pieces of Seraphina's life, something to explain the memories that had been haunting her nights.

In a drawer tucked beneath an old desk, she found a stack of yellowed papers bound with a faded ribbon. Her hands trembled slightly as she untied it, her curiosity outweighing her fear. As she sifted through the pages, one letter in particular caught her eye. The envelope was addressed to Mrs. Seraphina Blackwood, but it had never been opened, its seal still intact.

She hesitated, feeling as if she were about to intrude on something deeply personal. But something compelled her, an instinct urging her to uncover what lay within. She broke the seal carefully and unfolded the letter, the ink faded but still legible. Her eyes widened as she read the words, each line revealing a story far darker than she had imagined.

My dearest Seraphina,

There are truths we hide, even from those we love. I have long kept this from you, knowing the pain it would cause, but I can no longer live in silence. I can no longer pretend to be what you believe me to be.

I was not faithful to you. My heart, though it belonged to you once, faltered. There was another, one who brought me comfort in times I should have turned to you. I cannot explain why it happened, only that it did. I was weak, and I failed you. And now, I have lost you forever.

Please know that I never wished to hurt you, nor to betray the vows we made. But I was a man caught in my own fears, and in my folly, I wronged you in the most unforgivable way. The burden of this truth has weighed on me more heavily with each day, and now that I face the inevitable end, I can only hope that, in time, you might understand.

I do not ask for forgiveness; I know I do not deserve it. I only hope that you will one day find peace, beyond the hurt I have caused.

With the deepest regret,

Henry

Mara's hands trembled as she held the letter, her mind reeling. She felt the weight of each word, the raw sorrow and regret in Henry's confession. He had betrayed Seraphina, the woman who had loved him so deeply, the woman who had been driven to the edge of madness by his death, never knowing that his love had not been as steadfast as she believed.

Mara felt a surge of anger on Seraphina's behalf, a bitterness that mingled with her own sense of betrayal. All the rituals, the desperate attempts to bring him back, the nights filled with candlelight and whispered incantations—Seraphina had devoted herself to a man whose love had been tainted by lies. She had clung to his memory, unable to move on, not knowing that her devotion had been built on a false foundation.

But there was something more unsettling: the letter had never been read. It was still sealed, untouched until this very moment. Seraphina had gone to her grave believing that Henry had been wholly hers, that his absence was a cruel twist of fate, not the result of a fractured love. She had bound herself—and him—to the manor out of an all-consuming need to keep him close, not knowing that his heart had wandered.

The implications of this were devastating. Henry's spirit, which Seraphina had tried so desperately to tether to Blackwood Manor, might have remained because of guilt, a lingering regret that bound him as much as her own grief. And Seraphina, in her obsession, had trapped them both in a prison of betrayal and grief, neither able to let go.

Mara sank into a nearby armchair, the letter clutched in her hands, her mind racing with questions. She wondered if this knowledge might have changed anything, if it would have softened Seraphina's pain, allowed her to release him instead of clinging to a memory that was never as pure as she believed.

As she sat there, processing the letter's devastating contents, a strange sensation washed over her. The air in the library seemed to grow colder, heavier, pressing down on her like a weight. She felt the prickling sensation of being watched, and her eyes darted around the room, expecting to see a shadow in the corner or a figure standing in the doorway.

But the library was empty, silent save for the faint rustle of papers in her hands.

Yet Mara could sense a presence, a faint whisper of something angry, betrayed. It was as if Seraphina herself lingered, her spirit hovering over Mara, furious at the knowledge that had been kept from her, that had twisted her life into a bitter, desperate spiral.

Mara spoke softly, as though addressing the air around her, hoping her words might reach whatever presence seemed to be watching her.

"Seraphina... I'm sorry. I didn't know. I don't think you were ever meant to know."

But the coldness persisted, a chill that seemed to seep into her bones. She felt Seraphina's anguish in a way she never had before, an ache that pulsed through her like a living thing. Mara tried to imagine the agony of realizing that the person you had loved so fully, the person you had clung to beyond reason, had kept secrets from you, betrayed you.

The letter had revealed a truth that Seraphina had never had the chance to confront, a betrayal that had bound her to this place, anchoring her to the manor as much as the love she had lost. Mara wondered if this revelation had the power to change anything—or if it would simply deepen the widow's suffering, adding another layer to the torment that held her captive within the house.

As she sat there, the letter lying open in her lap, Mara felt an urgent need to return it to Seraphina's room, to place it with the other relics of her life and love, as if acknowledging this truth could somehow bring closure to the restless spirit.

With the letter carefully folded, Mara rose from the chair and left the library, her footsteps echoing through the empty hallways as she made her way to the east wing. The house felt different as she walked, a tension in the air, an almost watchful silence that seemed to follow her with every step.

When she reached Seraphina's room, she crossed the threshold with a reverent hesitation, as though entering a sacred place. She placed the letter on the vanity, beside the black veil and the delicate hand mirror, its cracked handle glinting faintly in the dim light.

As she laid the letter down, a sudden, overwhelming sadness filled her. She whispered into the stillness, a quiet plea to the woman whose life had been twisted by love and betrayal.

"Seraphina... he wasn't worth your suffering. You can let go now."

The silence around her deepened, a heavy stillness that seemed to press down on the room. For a moment, Mara thought she felt a shift in the air, a faint sigh, like a breath of wind passing through the closed room. But then it was gone, leaving only the quiet and the dim, lingering shadows.

Mara left the room, her heart heavy, unsure if her actions would make any difference to the restless spirits that roamed the halls of Blackwood Manor. But as she closed the door behind her, she felt as though a weight had lifted, if only slightly. She had uncovered the truth, and she had given it back to the woman who had been so cruelly denied it.

Yet, as she walked back to her room, she couldn't shake the feeling that the manor still held more secrets, layers of darkness woven into its walls, each one a fragment of Seraphina's broken heart.

The letter was only one piece of a tragedy that ran deeper than she had imagined. And Mara knew, with a certainty that chilled her, that Blackwood Manor would not rest until all its secrets were unearthed.

Chapter 13: The Forgotten Children

Days passed since Mara had uncovered the letter of betrayal, yet Blackwood Manor continued to feel restless, as though the revelation had stirred something deeper, something that lay buried beneath layers of grief and secrecy. The house seemed to breathe, to whisper, shadows shifting in the corners of her vision. She sensed it drawing her further, luring her into its depths with the promise of more answers, more pieces to the tragic story it was weaving around her.

One cold afternoon, Mara found herself once again in the attic. She had gone there on a whim, unable to resist the pull of the dark, cluttered space filled with remnants of the past. The attic was vast, its low beams draped with cobwebs, and the floor scattered with trunks, crates, and forgotten treasures, each one a silent testament to lives that had once filled the manor's walls with laughter and loss.

She moved carefully among the dust-covered trunks and boxes, her fingers trailing over the faded leather and peeling paint. A curious shape caught her eye—a small, ornate chest pushed back into the shadows, hidden beneath a stack of old blankets. It looked different from the other trunks, its wood carved with delicate patterns of ivy and roses, its lid locked with a rusty latch.

Mara pulled it forward, coughing as a cloud of dust erupted around her. She pried open the rusty latch with a faint creak and lifted the lid. Inside, she found what she least expected: tiny, forgotten relics of childhood.

A collection of small, well-worn toys lay scattered inside—a wooden horse, a tiny doll with one glass eye missing, a set of marbles in a small pouch. Beneath them lay folded pieces of clothing, faded and worn but meticulously preserved: a small woollen sweater, a delicate pair of shoes, and a baby's bonnet embroidered with pale blue thread.

The sight of these items sent a chill through her. She had never come across any mention of children in her exploration of the manor or Seraphina's life. Yet here they were, these intimate, delicate relics of a family long forgotten, tucked away in a hidden compartment as though they were secrets never meant to be found.

Her heart quickened as she examined each item, a strange feeling stirring within her. She couldn't help but imagine small, ghostly hands clutching the toys, little feet slipping into the shoes, soft laughter echoing in the halls. Yet, she knew that the presence of these items hinted at something darker. Why were they hidden away? Why had Seraphina—or someone else—kept them so carefully preserved, yet concealed?

She sifted through the chest, her fingers brushing against the fabric of a tiny dress stitched with flowers, each stitch lovingly made, each fold meticulously pressed. Beneath it, she found a small, weathered book, its cover worn and pages brittle with age. It was a diary, written in a scrawling, uneven hand that was unmistakably Seraphina's.

Mara opened the diary, her hands trembling as she flipped to the first entry. The writing was filled with a desperation she recognized from the other journals but with a tenderness she hadn't seen before.

April 3rd, 1891

Today was a happy day. Little Thomas took his first steps, and I felt my heart swell with pride. Henry was away, as usual, but I am content to watch our son grow, to see his bright eyes and know he is ours. My heart aches with love for him, my little one, my hope.

Mara's breath caught in her throat as she read. Thomas. Seraphina had a son—a child she had kept hidden, a child Mara had never read about in any of the widow's belongings. The joy in the words was evident, a fleeting happiness that felt out of place against the backdrop of sorrow and obsession that had marked Seraphina's life.

She continued reading, each entry hinting at the love and care Seraphina had poured into her child, her words filled with a gentle affection. But as Mara flipped further into the diary, the tone changed, growing darker, laced with sorrow and anxiety.

July 15th, 1892

Henry returned tonight. He did not even look at Thomas. His coldness has seeped into the walls, and I feel it pressing against us. He is angry, distant. He does not understand why I am here, why I have chosen to stay with our son. He talks of sending Thomas away, of what "people will say." But I cannot—I will not let him take my child from me.

A knot formed in Mara's stomach as she read. Henry had wanted to hide Thomas, to erase him from their lives, to protect the Blackwood reputation at the cost of their child. She could imagine the arguments that must have erupted between them, Seraphina clinging to her son, her only light amidst the shadows that had begun to creep into her life.

As Mara read further, her heart sank. The last entries were filled with despair, each one darker than the last.

October 21st, 1893

Thomas has taken ill. I can feel his little body weakening, see the light fading from his eyes. I pray each night, but it is no use. Henry remains distant, hardly caring as our son slips away. My heart is broken, shattered into pieces. I have given everything, yet I am losing him.

I will not let him go. I cannot let him leave me. I will find a way.

Mara closed her eyes, feeling the weight of Seraphina's grief pressing down on her, as if the widow's sorrow had seeped into her own heart. Thomas had been Seraphina's reason to live, her source of hope and light in an otherwise cold and lonely world. And now, she realized, the widow had tried to keep him as she had tried to keep Henry, desperately clinging to the lives she had lost.

Mara turned to the final entry, her hands shaking as she read Seraphina's last, desperate words:

October 29th, 1893

They have both left me. My heart is hollow, my world dark. I have tried to reach them, to bring them back, but the shadows remain silent.

I cannot escape this emptiness. My sweet Thomas... my beloved Henry. They are gone, and I am left alone in this prison of my own making.

If I cannot have them in life, I will have them in death.

The words sent a shiver through her, each one a bleak confirmation of what Mara had suspected. Seraphina had tried to hold onto them both, unable to release the past, unable to accept the losses that had torn her life apart. She had bound herself to Blackwood Manor, along with her memories, her pain, and the remnants of her love.

Mara set the diary down, her fingers brushing against the tiny sweater and shoes. She could feel the weight of Seraphina's love and loss filling the room, a sorrow so powerful it felt as if it could pull her into the shadows, into the endless void where the widow had imprisoned herself.

The attic grew colder, the shadows lengthening around her, and for a moment, Mara felt the faintest touch on her shoulder—a light, almost childlike touch that made her heart race. She glanced around, but the attic was empty, silent save for the faint creaks of the old house settling. Yet, she could sense something, an unseen presence watching her, waiting.

It was as if Seraphina's grief had conjured ghosts within the walls, phantoms of a life lost to sorrow and betrayal. Mara understood now that the widow had tried to save her son, to hold onto him even after death, but her efforts had left her bound to the house, her spirit forever searching, lingering, watching.

As she left the attic, clutching the diary to her chest, she felt the weight of those forgotten children, their toys and clothes silent echoes of a love that had never been allowed to flourish. Blackwood Manor was a place haunted not only by Seraphina's sorrow but by the shadows of those she had loved and lost.

And as Mara closed the door behind her, the faint sound of a child's laughter seemed to echo in the darkness, a ghostly memory drifting through the empty halls, a reminder that Blackwood Manor held far more than just its own secrets.

Chapter 14: The Ghostly Lullaby

That night, Blackwood Manor felt colder than usual, its silence heavy and unnerving, as if the house itself were bracing for something. Mara lay in bed, restless, her mind replaying the day's discoveries. The chest of children's belongings, the faded clothes and toys, and Seraphina's diary entries haunted her thoughts, painting a tragic portrait of a woman who had lost everything she loved.

As the clock struck midnight, a faint sound drifted through the darkness—a soft, haunting melody, the gentle strains of a lullaby. The sound was distant at first, a barely-there hum that seemed to linger at the edges of her hearing. But as she lay still, holding her breath, it grew louder, a delicate tune carrying through the empty halls.

Mara felt a chill slip down her spine. It was a lullaby she hadn't heard before, yet it felt familiar, as though it had always existed within the walls of the manor, waiting for this moment to reveal itself. The melody was gentle, hauntingly beautiful, tinged with a sadness that resonated deeply within her.

Compelled by a force she couldn't resist, Mara rose from her bed and wrapped herself in a shawl, her feet carrying her out of the room and into the darkened hallway. The melody grew clearer as she moved, each note floating through the air like a whispered memory, guiding her forward.

She followed the sound down the grand staircase, her footsteps silent against the worn floorboards. The house was draped in shadows, the moonlight casting faint, ghostly glimmers through the windows, illuminating dust motes that swirled in the cold air. The lullaby seemed to pulse, leading her through the corridors, winding deeper into the heart of Blackwood Manor.

As she neared the back entrance, the tune changed slightly, as if shifting with her steps, the notes twisting into a melancholy refrain that spoke of loss and love. She felt as though she were stepping into someone else's memory, her own thoughts blending with fragments of the past. It was as if the house itself were reaching out to her, guiding her, pushing her toward something she needed to see.

The sound drew her outside, into the garden. The night air was sharp and cold, the grounds cloaked in shadows and silence, save for the faint, ethereal melody that now seemed to come from somewhere within the overgrown garden. The moon hung low in the sky, casting a pale light over the twisted branches and unkempt paths, giving the garden a ghostly, dreamlike quality.

Mara moved through the tangled vines and overgrown hedges, the lullaby winding around her, luring her deeper into the darkness. She followed it instinctively, her heart pounding as she ventured further from the house, guided by the invisible hand of the past.

At the edge of the garden, in a forgotten corner beneath an old, gnarled tree, she saw it: a small patch of earth, slightly raised, as though it had been disturbed long ago. The ground was bare, the grass patchy and wilted, the soil dark and damp even in the moonlight. There was no headstone, no marker, just an unassuming mound of earth that seemed to blend into the shadows.

But Mara knew, in the deepest part of her heart, that this was a grave—a grave that had been left unmarked, forgotten.

The lullaby faded as she approached, the silence thickening around her, as if the very air were holding its breath. She knelt beside the grave, her fingers brushing the cold earth, feeling the sorrow that seemed to emanate from it. She could almost sense Seraphina's presence beside her, a grief-stricken mother keeping vigil over the resting place of her lost child.

A wave of sadness washed over Mara, filling her with a sorrow that wasn't entirely her own. She thought of the tiny clothes and toys she had found in the attic, the love and care that had gone into preserving them, as if they were all that remained of a life that had been stolen far too soon.

She whispered into the silence, her voice barely audible. "Thomas... was this your resting place?"

The night answered with silence, a silence that felt thick and ancient, filled with secrets that had been buried for generations. But as she knelt there, she felt the faintest brush of warmth against her hand, a fleeting sensation that felt almost like a child's hand resting atop her own. It was a comforting touch, soft and innocent, but tinged with a sadness that made her heart ache.

Mara closed her eyes, allowing the feeling to wash over her, sensing the presence of the child who had once lived within these walls. She thought of Seraphina's desperation, her attempts to hold onto her son even after death, her inability to accept the loss that had hollowed out her life. The widow's grief had seeped into every corner of the manor, binding it to the past, tethering both mother and child to the house in a tragic, unbreakable bond.

As Mara rose to leave, she felt a strange resolve take hold of her. She couldn't change the past, couldn't undo the suffering that had trapped Seraphina and her child in this endless loop of sorrow. But she could acknowledge it, honour it, bring to light the story that had been silenced for so long.

She looked down at the unmarked grave one last time, a quiet vow forming in her mind. "You won't be forgotten, Thomas. I promise."

The wind picked up slightly, stirring the leaves, and for a brief moment, Mara thought she heard the faintest echo of the lullaby, as though the spirit of the child were singing it softly, drifting through the night in a final goodbye.

She turned back toward the manor, her steps slow and deliberate as she moved through the overgrown paths. The house loomed in the distance, its dark silhouette against the pale light of the moon, watching her return with silent vigilance.

As she crossed the threshold back into Blackwood Manor, she felt a shift in the air, a faint sense of peace mingling with the familiar weight of the house's presence. She couldn't explain it, but she sensed that something had changed, that her discovery had soothed, if only slightly, the restless spirits that roamed the halls.

But as she made her way back to her room, Mara knew that this was only the beginning. The house still held its secrets tightly, shadows lurking in every corner, waiting to reveal themselves to her.

That night, as she drifted into a restless sleep, the lullaby continued to play softly in her mind, a ghostly reminder of the child whose memory had been hidden, but who now would no longer be forgotten. And though she felt a faint comfort in this, she knew that Blackwood Manor was far from finished with her—that the story of Seraphina, Thomas, and the legacy of love, loss, and betrayal was far from over.

The house had many more secrets to reveal. And Mara, bound by her own curiosity and compassion, would be there to uncover each and every one.

Chapter 15: The Attic Key

The following morning dawned grey and sombre, the light barely penetrating the heavy clouds that clung to the sky like a shroud. The discovery of the unmarked grave had weighed heavily on Mara's mind, filling her with both sorrow and a strange sense of resolve. She felt the urge to continue her search for answers, as if some invisible force within the house was propelling her forward, urging her to uncover its secrets.

After a sparse breakfast in the manor's drafty dining room, Mara made her way to the east wing, her steps echoing in the silent corridors. She found herself drawn to the widow's portrait, the haunting image that seemed to capture Seraphina's grief and bitterness in every stroke. Mara couldn't help but feel that this painting held more than just a likeness; it held a presence, a silent watchfulness that seemed almost alive.

She studied the portrait closely, taking in every detail. Seraphina's dark eyes seemed to follow her as she moved, and Mara couldn't shake the feeling that the widow was trying to tell her something, her gaze heavy with unspoken words. As she ran her fingers along the edge of the frame, she felt a slight unevenness beneath her fingertips, a small bulge hidden within the ornate moulding.

Curious, Mara pressed lightly against the frame, and to her surprise, a tiny compartment slid open at the bottom, revealing a small, rusted key nestled inside. It was delicate, wrought from dark metal with intricate etchings that seemed to catch the light in strange, almost sinister ways. She picked it up carefully, feeling the cool weight of it in her hand, her heart pounding with a mix of fear and exhilaration.

She knew immediately what this key was for. The attic.

Mrs. Havers had warned her from the beginning about the attic, forbidding her to venture there, hinting at dark relics and secrets that were best left untouched. But now, with the key in her hand, Mara felt as though she had been granted permission—perhaps even urged—to enter. She sensed that this was no accident, that the key had been left for her to find, hidden in the very portrait that seemed to embody Seraphina's spirit.

With a deep breath, Mara slipped the key into her pocket and made her way toward the narrow staircase that led to the attic. The air grew colder as she ascended, each step creaking beneath her weight, the silence thickening around her. She reached the attic door, a heavy, iron-bound barrier that looked as though it had not been opened in decades. Taking a steadying breath, she pulled the key from her pocket and inserted it into the lock, feeling the ancient mechanism resist before finally giving way with a soft, reluctant click.

The door swung open slowly, revealing a dark, cavernous space that stretched out before her. Dust floated in the air, shimmering in the faint light that seeped through a small, grimy window on the far wall. The attic was filled with shadows, the outlines of old furniture and forgotten trunks looming like spectres in the gloom.

Mara stepped inside, the air thick with the smell of mildew and age, as though the space had been sealed off from the world for generations. She closed the door behind her, the faint echo reverberating through the attic, and took a moment to let her eyes adjust to the dimness. As she moved deeper into the room, her gaze fell upon rows of strange, carefully arranged items, each one a relic from a time long past.

In one corner, an old cradle sat, its wood chipped and worn, a delicate lace blanket draped over the edge. Next to it was a rocking chair, its faded upholstery frayed and brittle, as though it had once been cherished but was now abandoned to the dust. Mara reached out, brushing her fingers along the armrest, feeling the faint echoes of lives that had once filled these rooms.

The further she explored, the stranger the items became. On a small, ornate table lay a collection of objects that seemed almost ritualistic in nature—a tarnished silver mirror, a bundle of dried herbs bound with a fraying ribbon, a series of candles that had long since melted down to stubs. In the center of the table sat a locket, its metal darkened with age, the initials S.B. engraved on its surface.

Mara hesitated, her fingers hovering over the locket. She could feel a strange energy radiating from it, a faint, pulsing warmth that seemed out of place in the cold, forgotten attic. She opened it slowly, her breath catching as she saw the tiny portrait inside—a young boy with a solemn expression, his eyes dark and hauntingly familiar.

Thomas.

She closed the locket gently, her heart heavy with the knowledge of Seraphina's lost child, the boy she had loved and mourned, the one she had tried so desperately to hold onto even beyond death. This attic was more than just a storage room; it was a shrine, a place where Seraphina had poured her sorrow, her love, her relentless need to keep her family close, even as they slipped away.

In the far corner of the attic, a faint glimmer caught her eye. She moved toward it, her pulse quickening as she saw what lay hidden beneath a draped sheet—a large mirror, its frame gilded and ornate, covered in delicate carvings of vines and flowers. The surface of the mirror was cracked in places, the glass warped and dark, but Mara felt drawn to it, an unexplainable pull that made her reach out to touch its surface.

As her fingers brushed the glass, an icy chill shot through her, and she felt a strange sensation, as though she were being drawn into the mirror itself. Her reflection stared back at her, but it was distorted, blurred, as if another face were layered over her own. She could make out Seraphina's features in the glass, her sorrowful eyes merging with Mara's, the boundaries between them fading, intertwining.

A sudden, vivid image flooded her mind—a memory not her own. She was standing in this very attic, the mirror before her, her hands trembling as she placed the locket at its base, whispering words of longing and loss. She could feel Seraphina's desperation, her need to keep her loved ones close, to bind them to her even as death threatened to take them away.

The memory faded, leaving Mara shaken, her heart pounding as she pulled her hand back from the mirror. She felt a sense of intrusion, as though she had glimpsed something forbidden, a moment of raw vulnerability that Seraphina had kept hidden within the attic, within the mirror itself.

She took a step back, her gaze lingering on the mirror, the distorted reflection that seemed to watch her, to plead with her. The attic felt colder now, the shadows deeper, as if the room itself had come alive, feeding off her fear, her curiosity. She knew that she had uncovered a piece of the house's dark history, a fragment of Seraphina's desperate attempts to defy death, to hold onto her family through whatever means necessary.

But she also knew that the manor had not yet revealed all its secrets.

As she turned to leave, a soft, almost inaudible whisper echoed through the attic, sending a shiver down her spine. It was Seraphina's voice, faint and broken, like a sigh carried on the wind.

"Help me... free us..."

The words lingered in the air, and Mara felt a deep, instinctive urge to turn back, to stay, to understand. But the shadows in the attic seemed to close in, the weight of Seraphina's grief pressing down on her, suffocating, relentless. She clutched the locket to her chest, the chill of the attic settling into her bones, a silent reminder of the house's tragic legacy.

As she stepped out of the attic and locked the door behind her, Mara knew that Blackwood Manor was demanding something of her. It was more than just a house filled with memories; it was a prison, a trap woven from love and sorrow, binding Seraphina and her family in a web of loss that had lingered for generations.

And now, Mara was a part of it.

Chapter 16: Signs of Possession

After her discovery in the attic, Mara felt an unsettling shift within herself, as though a thin, invisible thread now tied her to Blackwood Manor's tragic past. The key, the locket, the whispering plea from Seraphina—they lingered in her mind, haunting her waking thoughts and slipping into her dreams.

In the days that followed, Mara began to notice strange occurrences. It started subtly: a flicker in her reflection as she passed by a mirror, a shadow that didn't belong. She tried to dismiss it as a trick of the light or her mind playing tricks, but the sensation persisted, creeping into her consciousness with increasing intensity.

One afternoon, as she brushed her hair in front of the mirror in her bedroom, her hands slowed, a peculiar sensation washing over her. She felt disconnected, her movements foreign, as if she were watching herself from outside her own body. Her reflection held her gaze, her own eyes staring back at her, yet they looked somehow... different.

She leaned closer, studying her face. But her reflection didn't lean in with her. Instead, the figure in the mirror remained still, its gaze sharp and calculating, almost... sorrowful.

A chill ran down her spine, and she stepped back, her heart pounding as her reflection finally moved in sync with her. She let out a shaky breath, trying to steady herself, but the unsettling feeling clung to her, an eerie sense that something—or someone—was looking back at her, someone who wasn't entirely her.

That night, the sensation grew stronger. She found herself drawn to the manor's various mirrors, her footsteps guiding her almost unconsciously from one room to the next, each mirror casting her reflection in a way that felt hauntingly unnatural. She would catch glimpses of herself as she passed, but each time, her reflection seemed to hold a life of its own, her features shifting slightly, the dark eyes staring back with an intensity that left her breathless.

In the hallway, she stopped in front of a tall, gilded mirror, one that she had avoided since her arrival. Her reflection looked back at her, expression sombre, and as she stared, her face in the mirror began to change.

Her eyes darkened, her hair pulled back as though by unseen hands, her lips forming a thin, sad line. It was Seraphina's face staring back at her, the same haunted expression she had seen in the widow's portrait, but this time it was alive, moving, her gaze filled with a sadness so deep it felt as if it might swallow her whole.

Mara gasped, stumbling backward, her heart hammering as she tried to shake the image from her mind. She pressed her hands to her face, but when she lowered them, she saw her own reflection once again, unchanged, unremarkable. The hallway was silent, yet she couldn't shake the feeling that she was no longer alone, that the widow was watching her, lurking in the shadows, her presence woven into the very fabric of the house.

That night, the dreams returned, even more vivid and disturbing than before. In her dreams, she was Seraphina, wandering through the halls of Blackwood Manor, her footsteps echoing in the emptiness. She felt the widow's grief, her desperation, her bitterness—emotions so intense they felt as though they were burning through her.

In one dream, she found herself standing before the mirror in the attic, clutching the locket in her hand, her gaze hollow, her reflection a twisted, sorrowful version of herself. She could feel Seraphina's thoughts seeping into her mind, a torrent of memories and emotions, each one laced with a bitterness that clung to her like a poison. The sense of betrayal, the ache of loneliness, the unyielding need to cling to what had been lost—it all washed over her, filling her with a rage she couldn't explain.

When she awoke, her hands were trembling, her body drenched in cold sweat. She felt strange, disoriented, as though she hadn't fully returned from the dream. For a moment, as she lay there in the darkness, she felt as though she were Seraphina, trapped within her own sorrow, unable to break free from the confines of Blackwood Manor.

Over the next few days, the line between herself and Seraphina grew thinner, the widow's presence pressing into her mind, merging with her thoughts, her emotions. She would catch herself speaking words that weren't her own, thoughts creeping into her mind that felt foreign, filled with the kind of bitterness and despair that had plagued Seraphina's life.

One evening, as she stared into the mirror above her vanity, she felt the world tilt slightly, her vision blurring. She blinked, and suddenly, she was no longer in her own room, but in a version of it that felt older, darker, the walls lined with portraits she hadn't seen before. She was wearing a heavy black dress, her hands clasped tightly, and as she looked at herself in the mirror, she saw not Mara, but Seraphina staring back.

She tried to break free from the vision, to remind herself that she was Mara, but the feeling persisted, Seraphina's memories mingling with her own, a haze of sorrow and fury blurring her thoughts.

"Why did he betray me?" she heard herself whisper, the words slipping from her lips unbidden, laced with an anger that wasn't hers. The voice was her own, but the anguish behind it was Seraphina's, a voice from the past bleeding into the present, taking root within her.

In a sudden surge of terror, she broke away from the mirror, clutching the edge of the vanity as she fought to regain control of herself. She felt as though she were being pulled into the widow's memories, her own identity slipping, replaced by the fragments of a life consumed by betrayal and grief.

Desperate for clarity, Mara ran to the hallway, stumbling through the dimly lit corridors, each mirror reflecting a distorted, haunted version of herself, her face blending with Seraphina's, their expressions merging into a mask of sorrow.

She reached the end of the hall, where the largest mirror hung—a towering, ornate frame that seemed to swallow the light, casting her reflection in deep, shadowed tones. She stared at her face, watching as her features morphed, becoming Seraphina's once more, the widow's dark, hollow eyes filling with unshed tears, her mouth forming words that echoed in Mara's mind:

"Set me free."

Mara closed her eyes, her heart racing, the weight of Seraphina's sorrow pressing into her, filling her with a despair that felt endless. She felt her hands shake, her mind blurring as if she were no longer just herself but an echo, a shadow, bound to the house just as Seraphina had been.

When she finally opened her eyes, her reflection was her own once more, her face pale, her eyes wide with terror. She felt a wave of nausea, the world tilting around her as she clutched the wall for support, struggling to shake off the remnants of the possession that had clung to her.

Stumbling back to her room, Mara locked the door behind her, her breathing shallow, her hands still trembling. She sat on the edge of her bed, clutching her arms to steady herself, the echo of Seraphina's presence lingering, a shadow that seemed to cling to her skin, to her very soul.

The house was pulling her deeper, blurring the boundaries between past and present, between herself and the ghostly spirit that haunted Blackwood Manor. She had seen Seraphina's face in her own, had felt the widow's despair pressing into her, merging with her thoughts.

And as she sat there, the darkness of the room pressing in around her, Mara knew with chilling certainty that Blackwood Manor was far from finished with her. The house had begun to possess her, to pull her into its web of sorrow and madness, piece by piece.

And as much as she wanted to resist, Mara feared that she was already too far gone.

Chapter 17: Shadows in the Mirror

The days had taken on a surreal, dreamlike quality for Mara. The boundaries between herself and Seraphina grew thinner, the widow's memories and emotions seeping into her consciousness, distorting her sense of reality. Each time she looked into a mirror, she braced herself, fearing what she might see. But curiosity, or perhaps the pull of the house itself, compelled her to look, to confront the reflections that seemed to hold more than just her own image.

One evening, after another restless day in Blackwood Manor, Mara found herself once more in front of the tall mirror in the hallway, the largest and most imposing of them all. The frame's intricate carvings twisted and spiralled like tangled vines, wrapping around the mirror as if protecting whatever secrets it held within. She stood there, almost mesmerized, watching her reflection as it stared back at her, expression blank, her face pale and drawn.

She studied her reflection, her gaze lingering on her own eyes. But even as she tried to ground herself, a strange movement caught her attention. In the mirror, shadows began to shift behind her, dark forms taking shape just at the edges of her reflection, flickering and shifting like smoke.

Her pulse quickened as she focused on the shadows, feeling a chill creep up her spine. The figures were indistinct at first, blurred shapes that seemed to hover, watching her. She felt her breath catch as one of the shadows moved closer, its form sharpening slightly, taking on the faint outline of a person.

A chill washed over her, and her hands clenched at her sides. She resisted the urge to turn around, knowing somehow that if she looked away, the figures would vanish. Instead, she kept her gaze locked on the mirror, watching as the shadowy figures multiplied, each one lingering behind her, each one watching her with an intensity that made her skin crawl.

The shadows began to take on faces—faces she recognized from the portraits scattered throughout the manor. They were the Blackwood's, generations of them, their expressions solemn, filled with the same sadness, the same quiet resentment that haunted the halls of Blackwood Manor. She saw a tall man with piercing eyes, a woman with delicate features and a grim expression, and even a child, his face round and pale, his eyes hollow.

But the shadow that drew her attention the most was the last one to appear, drifting forward until it stood directly behind her. It was Seraphina.

In the mirror, the widow's face was a mask of sorrow and bitterness, her dark eyes fixed on Mara's reflection. Mara's heart pounded as she felt Seraphina's presence draw closer, a suffocating weight pressing into her, filling the air with an oppressive energy. The widow's lips moved, forming words Mara couldn't hear, her expression one of desperation, as if she were trying to communicate something urgent, something that lay trapped within the confines of the mirror.

Unable to resist, Mara whispered, "What do you want?"

The reflection of Seraphina leaned forward, her face almost merging with Mara's own in the mirror. The shadows deepened, swirling around them, and Mara felt the cold brush of something intangible, like an invisible hand grazing her shoulder.

"Free me..."

The words echoed faintly, a whisper so soft it was barely audible, yet they resonated deep within her, chilling her to the core. Mara's gaze remained fixed on Seraphina's reflection, her heart pounding as the widow's eyes bore into hers, filled with a pleading desperation.

But just as Mara opened her mouth to respond, another movement caught her eye. The child's face, the same pale, haunting figure she'd seen in her dreams, drifted closer, his hollow gaze piercing through her. He seemed to reach for her, his small hand extending toward her reflection in the mirror, his eyes filled with an innocence laced with sorrow.

The shadows around him moved as if alive, swirling and shifting, their forms blurring, merging into one another, their faces fading and reappearing as if caught in a perpetual cycle of suffering.

The sight was too much. Mara finally turned around, breaking her gaze from the mirror, her breath coming in shallow, panicked gasps. She expected to see the hallway empty, the figures vanished, as they always did. But this time, as she looked behind her, she thought she caught a faint flicker—a shadow darting just out of view, vanishing around the corner.

Her skin prickled with fear. The shadows were not confined to the mirror anymore; they were here, in the house, lingering just out of sight.

She turned back to the mirror, but her reflection looked ordinary, tired and shaken, her face pale with fear. The shadows were gone, leaving only the still, silent corridor behind her.

Mara backed away from the mirror, her heart racing, a deep sense of unease settling over her. The figures hadn't been a mere hallucination or a figment of her imagination. They were real, or as real as the restless spirits that haunted Blackwood Manor could be. She felt as though the house itself had allowed her a glimpse into its tortured past, revealing the shadows that lingered within its walls, spirits bound by secrets and sorrows that spanned generations.

But Seraphina's words echoed in her mind, a plea that lingered like a dark stain on her thoughts.

Free me.

The request weighed heavily on her, filling her with a sense of dread and responsibility she hadn't anticipated. Seraphina was trapped here, bound by the grief and bitterness that had consumed her in life, her spirit lingering in the shadows, unable to find peace.

Mara felt a chill settle into her bones as she realized the full extent of what was being asked of her. The house wanted her to do more than uncover its secrets. It wanted her to release them, to unbind the spirits that had woven themselves into its very walls.

But how? How could she free Seraphina and the others from a prison built from memories, bound by emotions so powerful they had transcended death?

She left the mirror and retreated to her room, locking the door behind her, her mind racing with questions. As she lay in bed, her thoughts a tangled mess of images and memories, she couldn't shake the sensation that the shadows were watching her, lingering just beyond the edge of sight, waiting for her to fulfil the widow's desperate plea.

That night, Mara dreamed again. She was in the hallway, standing before the same mirror, but this time, the shadows surrounded her, their faces watching, silent and expectant. She felt Seraphina's hand on her shoulder, cold and unyielding, her voice a whisper in the darkness.

"The house holds us... but it cannot hold you."

Mara woke with a start, Seraphina's words ringing in her ears, her heart racing as she lay there, staring into the darkened room. She felt as though a weight had settled over her, a responsibility she hadn't asked for yet could not ignore.

Blackwood Manor was more than just a haunted house. It was a prison, a place where memories and spirits lingered, bound by the unresolved pain and sorrow that had soaked into its walls.

And somehow, Mara knew, she was the key.

In the quiet darkness of her room, Mara made a silent vow. She would uncover the truth of Blackwood Manor, whatever it took. She would find a way to free the spirits bound within its walls, to release them from the shadows that held them captive.

For the first time since arriving, she felt a glimmer of determination, a purpose to guide her through the darkness.

But as she drifted back to sleep, she knew that the house would not make it easy.

And somewhere in the shadows, Seraphina watched, waiting.

Chapter 18: Unseen Visitors

The atmosphere in Blackwood Manor had grown heavier, as if the house itself sensed Mara's resolve to uncover its secrets and free the spirits that clung to it. The air was thick with an energy she could almost taste, a tension that seemed to vibrate through the walls, the floors, even the very furniture. Mara could feel it everywhere—she was no longer merely a guest here; she was part of the house's story, woven into its tapestry of sorrow and loss.

It began with faint murmurs, the kind that fluttered at the edge of hearing, like a distant conversation carried on a breeze. The voices came most often at night, rising and falling in low, muffled tones, the words just beyond comprehension. Mara would lie in bed, listening, her heart pounding as the voices filled the silence, fading just as she strained to make out what they were saying.

One evening, as she sat in the library attempting to read by candlelight, she heard the faint sound of laughter echoing from somewhere deep within the manor. It was soft, ghostly, like the laughter of children playing in distant rooms. The sound startled her, and she froze, her book slipping from her hands. She glanced around, but the room was empty, the only movement the flickering shadows cast by the candle flame.

The laughter died away, replaced by a hush that seemed to settle over the house, a silence so complete it was almost oppressive. But Mara couldn't shake the feeling that she was no longer alone, that unseen eyes were watching her, lingering in the dark corners of the room.

Compelled by a strange, restless curiosity, she left the library and wandered through the halls, her footsteps soft against the floor. The house was silent, its darkened corridors empty, but she could feel an invisible presence moving alongside her, brushing against her, a faint pressure against her skin, like hands reaching out but never quite touching.

As she passed a large window overlooking the garden, she thought she saw movement out of the corner of her eye—a faint outline, the silhouette of a woman in a long, flowing dress, standing by the fountain. Mara stopped, her breath catching, and turned to look, but the garden was empty, the moon casting an eerie light over the tangled branches and darkened statues.

She continued down the hallway, her heart racing, her senses heightened. She felt as if she were walking through a memory, a world layered over her own, each shadow and echo a fragment of lives that had once filled these walls. The hallway seemed to stretch and contract around her, the edges blurring as if the house itself were shifting, transforming, creating space for the phantoms that lingered within.

At the end of the hall, she saw a faint outline, a figure standing by a door. It was a woman, her form hazy, almost transparent, but unmistakably there. Mara could make out the details of her dress, the long, flowing skirt and lace sleeves, her hair pinned up in an old-fashioned style. The figure didn't turn to face her but instead stood with her head bowed, her posture one of sorrow, of resignation.

"Seraphina?" Mara whispered, her voice trembling.

The figure shifted slightly, as if hearing her, but didn't turn. Mara took a step closer, her heart pounding, the weight of the house pressing down on her as if daring her to reach out. But as she extended her hand, the figure dissolved into mist, leaving only the faintest whisper in the air, a sigh that faded into silence.

Her pulse quickened, a strange mixture of fear and fascination gripping her as she stood alone in the hallway, the empty air heavy with the presence of those who had come before. She moved carefully, making her way toward the grand staircase, feeling as though she were walking through a veil that separated her world from theirs.

As she descended the stairs, she saw other figures—flickers of movement in her periphery, shapes that seemed to solidify for a brief moment before vanishing again. She saw a man in a dark suit standing by the fireplace, his face turned toward the flames, lost in thought. A young girl in a white dress, her hair tied with a ribbon, sat on the bottom step of the staircase, her expression solemn and her eyes fixed on something Mara couldn't see.

The voices grew louder, filling the space around her. She could hear snippets of conversations, laughter, even the soft strains of a piano playing somewhere in the distance, its melody haunting and familiar, as if it were a song she had known in another life.

Mara felt as though she were slipping between worlds, moving through a memory that was as real as the present, each figure a part of Blackwood Manor's past, each one bound to the house by some unbreakable tether. She realized, with a chilling certainty, that these were the long-dead inhabitants of Blackwood Manor, their spirits lingering in the house, trapped within its walls, unable—or perhaps unwilling—to leave.

Her steps slowed as she reached the grand salon, where the voices seemed to converge, filling the room with a cacophony of whispers and laughter, faint echoes of conversations from lives long past. She could see outlines of figures moving through the space, a ghostly gathering of people dressed in clothes from different eras, their faces indistinct but filled with emotion—sadness, joy, anger, despair.

At the center of the room, she saw Seraphina's figure, her form more solid than the others, her face shadowed yet unmistakable. She stood silently, watching the other figures with an expression of deep sorrow, her hands clasped in front of her as if in silent mourning.

Mara felt a wave of empathy wash over her. She could sense the weight of Seraphina's grief, the bitterness that had kept her bound to this place, unable to let go. The voices around her grew louder, a chaotic symphony of emotions that pulsed through the room, pressing down on her, filling her with a despair that wasn't entirely her own.

"Why do you linger here?" Mara whispered, her voice trembling.

Seraphina's figure turned, her face pale and solemn, her dark eyes filled with a sadness so deep it seemed to radiate from her very being. She moved closer, her gaze locking onto Mara's, and for a moment, Mara felt as though she could see directly into the widow's soul, a glimpse of the pain and betrayal that had consumed her in life, binding her to the manor even in death.

"We cannot leave," Seraphina's voice whispered, though her lips did not move. The words echoed in Mara's mind, a faint, haunting plea that filled her with a cold, unshakable dread.

"Why?" Mara asked, her voice barely above a whisper.

The voices around her grew softer, a hush settling over the room as Seraphina's figure seemed to flicker, her form blurring as if caught between worlds.

"Because the house remembers," Seraphina's voice answered, her tone filled with a bitterness that cut through the silence. "It holds our memories, our pain, our regrets. We are woven into its walls, bound by the shadows of what we once were."

Mara felt a tear slip down her cheek, the weight of Seraphina's words sinking into her. The house was more than just a place; it was a prison of memories, a vessel for the sorrows and secrets of those who had lived and died within its walls.

The figures around her began to fade, their outlines dissolving into mist, their voices fading into silence. But as Seraphina's figure vanished, her gaze lingered on Mara, a silent, pleading look that spoke of a desperation that transcended death.

"Free us," Seraphina's voice echoed, a faint whisper that lingered in the air even as her form disappeared.

Mara stood alone in the grand salon, the silence pressing down on her like a weight. She knew, with a chilling certainty, that Blackwood Manor held its inhabitants captive, their spirits bound by the memories that had seeped into its very foundation.

As she made her way back to her room, her heart heavy with the knowledge of what she had seen, she felt a newfound determination settle over her. She would find a way to free them, to release the spirits that lingered within Blackwood Manor, to bring peace to those who had been trapped by the shadows of their past.

But deep down, Mara knew that the house would not let them go easily. It held its secrets tightly, a web woven from sorrow and regret, and she was only just beginning to untangle its threads.

And as she drifted into an uneasy sleep, the voices continued to whisper, filling the silence with a quiet, haunting plea.

Free us.

Chapter 19: The Widow's Secret Room

Mara awoke with a renewed sense of purpose, though her dreams had left her feeling haunted, the whispers and shadowy figures lingering in her mind. She could still hear the faint plea echoing in her ears—Free us. The spirits of Blackwood Manor were trapped, bound to the house by sorrow, regret, and something darker. But beneath the despair, she sensed a flicker of hope, as if the manor itself were guiding her toward something that could help her uncover its secrets.

As she moved through the house that day, a restless curiosity took hold of her. She had explored most of Blackwood Manor, but she couldn't shake the feeling that there were still hidden corners, places the house had kept concealed from her. Determined to uncover whatever the manor was hiding, Mara began to search the rooms more carefully, her eyes scanning every detail, her fingers trailing along the walls, feeling for anything unusual.

Her search led her to the east wing, where the atmosphere felt different, colder, almost as if the house were holding its breath. She moved slowly down the hallway, her steps soft, her senses alert. She came to a heavy, wooden panel at the far end of the corridor, one she hadn't paid much attention to before. But now, she felt drawn to it, an instinctual pull that urged her to investigate further.

Gently pressing her hand against the panel, Mara felt a faint vibration, as though something within the wall was waiting to be revealed. She pushed harder, and to her surprise, the panel shifted slightly, revealing a narrow crack that ran vertically along the edge. Her heart quickened as she pulled the panel open, revealing a hidden passageway that spiralled down into darkness.

Taking a deep breath, she stepped into the passage, the air growing colder with each step. The narrow staircase descended steeply, the walls lined with faded wallpaper that looked older than anything else in the house. The air was thick with dust, and Mara had to stifle a cough as she moved deeper, her heart pounding with a mixture of fear and excitement.

At the bottom of the staircase, she found herself in a small, dimly lit room, the light filtering in through a narrow, barred window high up on the wall. The room had an oppressive stillness, a quiet that felt almost sacred, as though it had been untouched for years. The air was filled with the faint, musty smell of age, tinged with a metallic scent that made her uneasy.

The room was unlike any other she had seen in Blackwood Manor. The walls were lined with ritualistic symbols, drawn in dark, fading ink. Strange, twisted shapes and ancient sigils covered nearly every surface, each one radiating an energy that made her skin prickle. In the center of the room was a low, wooden table, its surface cluttered with personal belongings—objects that looked intimately familiar, as though they had once belonged to Seraphina herself.

Mara moved closer, her eyes scanning the items on the table: a tarnished locket, an ivory hair comb, a bundle of dried lavender bound with a frayed ribbon. Each item felt significant, imbued with a personal weight that spoke of Seraphina's life, her memories, her secrets. Among the items, she found a small, worn book, its leather cover cracked and peeling with age. She opened it carefully, the brittle pages covered in Seraphina's handwriting, her words filled with a desperate intensity.

July 19th, 1893

The rituals are my only hope now. I have tried everything else, prayed, begged, pleaded with forces I do not understand. But Henry's spirit remains elusive, slipping through my fingers like smoke. The house holds him, I know it does, yet he is beyond my reach. I must go further, deeper into the old ways, no matter the cost.

Mara felt a shiver as she read, sensing the desperation that had driven Seraphina to explore darker, more forbidden paths. She flipped through the pages, her fingers trembling as she read passages detailing Seraphina's attempts to reach Henry, to bind him to the house, to bring him back to her. Each entry grew darker, more frantic, her words a descent into madness.

October 1st, 1893

I have made contact, but it is not as I expected. His presence is there, lingering in the shadows, but it is twisted, warped, as though something has corrupted him. He is bound to the house now, yet he remains... incomplete. I fear I have taken something that cannot be returned, that he is no longer the man I loved.

Mara's hands shook as she closed the book, the implications of Seraphina's actions settling heavily on her. The widow's desperation had led her to a place of darkness, binding her husband's spirit to the house, but in doing so, she had only succeeded in trapping him in a twisted, tormented state. And now, it seemed, her own spirit was bound to the manor as well, a prisoner of her own making.

Her gaze fell on the walls, the symbols seeming to pulse faintly in the dim light. She reached out, tracing one of the sigils with her fingers, feeling a faint, tingling warmth radiate from it. She recognized some of the symbols from her research into occult practices, but others were unfamiliar, more ancient and complex, each one etched with a precision that spoke of Seraphina's dedication.

In one corner of the room, she noticed a larger symbol—a circle drawn with dark, smudged lines, its center filled with smaller, interconnected shapes. Inside the circle lay a ring of dried flowers, their petals crumbling to dust, and a single, weathered candle that looked as though it had been burned down to a stump. She felt an instinctual aversion to the symbol, sensing that it was the focal point of Seraphina's rituals, a doorway to the other side.

Compelled by a force she didn't fully understand, Mara knelt beside the circle, her fingers brushing the edge of the symbol. As she touched it, a sudden wave of memories washed over her, images flooding her mind—Seraphina, standing in this very room, chanting softly, her voice filled with longing and despair. She saw Henry's shadow flickering in the corner, a twisted, ghostly form reaching out to her, yet forever out of reach.

A whisper filled the air, faint and broken, as if carried from a great distance. It was Seraphina's voice, filled with sorrow and regret.

"I tried... but I only made it worse..."

Mara felt a tear slip down her cheek, the weight of Seraphina's words settling over her like a shroud. She understood now that the widow had been trapped by her own choices, bound to the house by the very rituals she had performed to save herself from the pain of loss. She had wanted to keep her family close, but in her desperation, she had bound them to a prison of memories and shadows.

As Mara rose, her gaze fell on a small, intricately carved box hidden beneath a layer of dust on a shelf in the corner. She picked it up, opening it slowly. Inside lay a piece of paper, brittle with age, covered in symbols similar to those on the walls. It was a ritual—a reversal, a way to undo what had been done, to break the bonds that held Seraphina and her family captive.

Her heart pounded as she studied the symbols, the instructions written in Seraphina's handwriting. This was it—the key to freeing them, to releasing the spirits that lingered within Blackwood Manor.

But as she held the paper, the air grew colder, and she felt a presence settle over the room, a weight that pressed down on her, filling her with an unshakable sense of dread. She knew, with a bone-deep certainty, that the house would not let go easily, that whatever darkness Seraphina had called upon had seeped into the very foundation of the manor, binding it as tightly as the spirits within.

Taking the paper and the small ritual box, Mara left the room, her steps slow and careful, feeling as though she were leaving a sanctuary filled with the sorrow of a life shattered by desperation. As she closed the hidden door behind her, she felt a final whisper drift through the air, Seraphina's voice faint but clear, filled with a hope that cut through the silence.

"Free us, Mara... please."

Back in the dim hallway, Mara clutched the paper to her chest, feeling the weight of the responsibility settle over her. She had the means to break the curse, to release the spirits bound to Blackwood Manor. But she knew it would not be easy. The house would resist, its darkness clinging to every corner, every shadow, fighting to keep its hold over those it had claimed.

Yet, as she made her way back to her room, a fierce determination filled her. She would perform the ritual, would free Seraphina, Henry, Thomas, and the others who lingered in torment.

And though the house loomed around her, filled with shadows and whispers, Mara knew that she was not alone. The spirits of Blackwood Manor were with her, waiting, watching, hoping for the peace they had been denied for so long.

With the ritual paper in hand, Mara braced herself for what lay ahead. She was prepared to confront the darkness, to face the weight of Blackwood Manor's tragic past, and, finally, to set them free.

Part III: The Web Tightens
Chapter 20: The Curse Unveiled

The next morning, Mara sat alone in the library, the ritual paper and Seraphina's journal laid out before her. The night had been restless, filled with whispers that tugged at the edges of her dreams, shadows that seemed to shift and writhe as if alive. She could feel the house's presence, its resistance to her discovery, an almost sentient awareness that seemed to coil around her, thick and suffocating.

With a steadying breath, she opened Seraphina's journal once more, flipping to the later entries, hoping for answers that would help her understand the curse and what it would take to break it. The ink on these pages was darker, more jagged, the words scrawled with a frantic, unsteady hand. The descent into despair was evident, each line filled with a desperation that clung to Mara's heart, squeezing it with a pressure that felt almost unbearable.

October 3rd, 1893

I have bound them all here, all who betrayed me, all who have turned a blind eye to my suffering. This house will keep them, hold them, as it holds me. It is their punishment and my salvation. None shall leave these walls while I remain.

Mara's heart pounded as she read, realization settling over her. Seraphina had enacted the curse herself, binding not only her husband and child but anyone tied to the manor, their souls trapped within its walls. It wasn't merely grief or love that kept them there; it was the widow's own rage and heartbreak, woven into the very foundation of Blackwood Manor.

She continued reading, each entry darker than the last, filled with Seraphina's anger and resentment. It became clear that, in her grief, Seraphina had blamed not only Henry but everyone connected to him—the family members, the servants, even distant relatives who hadn't intervened. She saw their indifference as complicity, and in her mind, they were all guilty.

The curse was a prison, one Seraphina had created not only to keep Henry close but to force the souls she believed had wronged her to suffer alongside her, bound to Blackwood Manor until the end of time.

October 10th, 1893

They move in the shadows, they whisper to me, but I hold the power. I have bound them here with my sorrow, with my rage, with my love that has soured. They are mine, as is this house. I am the keeper, the warden, and none shall be free.

Mara's hands trembled as she closed the journal, the magnitude of what Seraphina had done pressing down on her. The widow's pain had transformed into something darker, a need for vengeance that had twisted her love and sorrow into a curse that reached beyond the grave.

But beneath the anger, Mara sensed something else—regret, perhaps even guilt. She remembered the whispers she had heard, the glimpses of Seraphina's ghostly form in the mirrors, the plea that had lingered in the air: Free us. Seraphina's spirit was trapped as well, bound by the very curse she had enacted, unable to escape the cycle of suffering she had created.

Mara felt a deep sadness welling up within her, mingling with her own determination. She had uncovered the truth, the reason why the spirits were bound to Blackwood Manor, but the path to freeing them remained uncertain. The curse was woven into the fabric of the house, a tapestry of sorrow and vengeance that seemed almost alive, feeding off the pain it had caused.

But the ritual paper, the reversal instructions she had found in the hidden room, offered a glimmer of hope.

The steps were simple, yet profound, calling for a release of the emotions that bound the souls to the house—a symbolic act of letting go, of forgiveness, something that would break the chains of resentment and allow the spirits to find peace. She would need to speak each name aloud, acknowledging their pain, asking for their forgiveness, and, most importantly, offering Seraphina the release she had denied herself in life.

But as she prepared herself, Mara knew it would not be an easy task. The house would resist, would fight to keep the spirits within its walls, clinging to the curse that had sustained it for so long. She had felt its resistance, its dark energy tightening around her with every step she took toward uncovering the truth.

Steeling herself, Mara stood and gathered the ritual paper, the journal, and a small candle. She knew the ritual had to take place in the heart of the house, the place where the curse was strongest. Her steps led her instinctively to the grand salon, the room where she had seen the ghostly figures gather, where Seraphina had once stood, filled with a grief that had transformed into something deadly.

The air grew colder as she entered the room, her footsteps echoing in the silence. Shadows flickered at the edges of her vision, but she ignored them, lighting the candle and setting it in the center of the room. She unfolded the ritual paper, her hands trembling as she prepared to speak the words, the instructions etched into her mind.

Taking a deep breath, she began, her voice steady, though her heart raced with a mixture of fear and resolve.

"I call upon the spirits of Blackwood Manor," she said, her voice reverberating through the empty room. "I know of your suffering, your pain, your sorrow. I know you have been bound here by grief and by anger, by a love that turned to vengeance."

She paused, feeling the air grow denser, as though the very walls were listening, watching, waiting.

"Seraphina," she continued, her voice softening, "you have held them here, and you have held yourself here, bound by the weight of your grief. But it is time to let go, to release the pain that ties you to this place."

The candle flickered, casting strange shadows on the walls. Mara felt a chill pass through her, as though invisible hands were reaching out, touching her skin with a cold, lingering sadness.

She spoke each name, calling upon the spirits who lingered in the house, her voice gentle yet firm. With every name, she felt a weight lift, a sense of release that seemed to ripple through the air, faint but undeniable.

When she reached Seraphina's name, she hesitated, her voice catching as she felt the widow's presence pressing in around her, filled with a sadness that seemed to stretch across the years, endless and consuming.

"Seraphina Blackwood," she said, her voice barely above a whisper, "I release you. I release you from the anger, the sorrow, the regret. You have suffered, and you have made others suffer, but it is time to let go."

The room grew colder, the candle flame guttering, as though resisting her words. But Mara continued, pouring her own compassion into the ritual, hoping it would reach the widow's spirit, that it would pierce through the darkness that had bound her for so long.

"You are free," Mara whispered, a tear slipping down her cheek. "You are free to leave, to find peace, to release the chains that have held you here."

The candle flame flickered wildly, and for a moment, Mara felt a presence beside her—a faint, ghostly figure that seemed to hover in the corner of her vision. She turned, and there was Seraphina, her face softened, her eyes filled with a mixture of sorrow and relief.

The widow's lips moved, forming words that Mara could barely hear, but the message was clear.

"Thank you."

And then, as quickly as she had appeared, Seraphina's figure dissolved into the shadows, her form fading into a wisp of light that floated upward, merging with the flickering candle flame before vanishing entirely.

The room grew silent, a profound stillness settling over it, as though the very essence of the house had shifted, lightened. The darkness that had filled Blackwood Manor, the shadows and whispers, seemed to recede, leaving only an echo of peace in their wake.

Mara extinguished the candle, her heart filled with a quiet sense of triumph and sadness. She had done it. She had freed the spirits, released them from the prison of memories and regret that had bound them to Blackwood Manor for so long.

As she made her way back through the empty halls, the silence felt different, no longer oppressive but peaceful, as though the house itself had finally been unburdened. She knew that the spirits were gone, that Seraphina and the others had found the release they had so desperately needed.

And as she crossed the threshold of Blackwood Manor for the last time, Mara felt a faint breeze brush against her cheek, a gentle, silent farewell from those she had freed.

Blackwood Manor was no longer haunted. The curse had been lifted, and its inhabitants had found peace at last.

Chapter 21: Trapped Inside

The silence in Blackwood Manor was almost overwhelming, a stillness that pressed down on Mara as she made her way toward the front door. She had done it—she had broken the curse, freed the spirits, released Seraphina and the others from the web of grief and rage that had bound them for so long. She could feel it in the air, the heavy tension that had filled the house replaced with a lightness, a calm that had never been there before.

But as she reached the door, her heart pounding with relief, something felt wrong. She twisted the brass handle, but it didn't move. Frowning, she tried again, pressing her weight against the door, but it refused to budge, as if something held it shut from the other side.

Mara felt a chill creep over her, a familiar dread tightening in her chest. She tried the handle again, pulling with all her strength, but the door remained immovable, locked as if by some unseen force.

A flicker of fear sparked in her mind. She turned, moving quickly through the house, checking every door, every window, her desperation mounting with each failed attempt. The windows were barred, the doors locked, all of them unyielding, as though the house itself had closed in around her, trapping her within its walls.

"Hello?" she called out, her voice echoing in the empty halls. "Is anyone here?"

Her voice was met with silence, the emptiness of the manor pressing down on her, growing heavier with each passing moment. She moved through room after room, her footsteps growing frantic as she searched for a way out. But every exit was blocked, every escape route barred, as if Blackwood Manor had sealed itself shut.

Panic rose in her throat, and she pressed her hand to her chest, willing herself to stay calm. She had freed the spirits; she had completed the ritual. The house should have been at peace, should have released her along with the others. So why did it feel as though she were still bound, held captive by something she couldn't see?

She stopped in front of a large mirror in the hallway, her reflection pale, her eyes wide with fear. As she stared, she thought she saw something move in the shadows behind her, a faint flicker that made her skin prickle.

"Who's there?" she whispered, her voice barely audible.

In the mirror, her reflection remained still, watching her, but the shadows seemed to shift, coiling around her like a dark, silent presence. She turned, but the hallway was empty, the house silent, yet the sensation of being watched persisted, pressing in on her, filling her with a growing sense of dread.

It was as if the house itself were alive, sentient, its walls breathing, watching, waiting.

Mara took a deep breath, trying to steady herself. Think, Mara. There must be a way out.

She returned to the grand salon, the room where she had performed the ritual, hoping to find some clue, some lingering trace of the spirits she had freed. But the room was empty, the candle extinguished, the air thick with the scent of smoke and something else—something darker, metallic, like blood and ash.

A faint whisper drifted through the room, so soft it was barely there, a sound that sent a chill down her spine.

"Stay…"

Mara's heart skipped a beat, and she looked around, her eyes scanning the shadows, but there was no one there. She felt a cold hand brush her arm, a sensation so real it made her gasp, and she stumbled back, her pulse racing.

"No," she whispered, backing away. "No, I did everything. I freed you. You're supposed to be at peace."

But the whisper came again, louder this time, filling the empty space around her, a voice that seemed to resonate from the walls themselves.

"Stay... with us..."

The shadows began to shift, pooling around her feet, stretching up along the walls, dark tendrils that twisted and writhed, as though the house were reaching out to pull her back. Mara tried to move, but her feet felt rooted to the floor, held in place by an unseen force.

Her mind raced, her thoughts spiralling as she struggled to understand. She had lifted the curse, she was certain of it. But perhaps in doing so, she had bound herself to the house, taking on the burden that had been lifted from the spirits. Perhaps Blackwood Manor had claimed her in their place, trapping her within its walls as payment for the release she had granted them.

Desperation filled her, and she fought against the invisible force that held her, her voice trembling as she called out, "Seraphina! Henry! Anyone—please, help me!"

But there was no answer, only the deep, suffocating silence that seemed to press down on her, filling her with a terror that made her heart pound. The shadows continued to creep up the walls, twisting into strange shapes, faces that seemed to leer at her, their expressions twisted with a cruel satisfaction.

Mara felt tears prick her eyes as she realized the truth. Blackwood Manor was never merely a haunted house. It was something darker, something alive, a force that fed on grief, on despair, on the souls of those who had walked its halls. And now, with the spirits freed, it had turned its attention to her, binding her to itself as it had bound them.

"No," she whispered, shaking her head, her voice filled with a desperate defiance. "I won't stay. I won't let you trap me here."

But even as she spoke, she felt the weight of the house pressing down on her, pulling her deeper into its embrace, its presence surrounding her, filling her mind with whispers that twisted and echoed, each one urging her to surrender, to give in, to stay.

Stay... Stay with us...

Mara stumbled back, her hands pressing against the walls as she fought to hold on to herself, to resist the pull that threatened to consume her. She had come to Blackwood Manor to uncover its secrets, to free the souls that had been trapped within its walls. But now, as the shadows closed in around her, she realized that she had become part of its story, another lost soul bound to the house's dark legacy.

She closed her eyes, her mind racing as she tried to think of a way out, some loophole in the curse, some way to break the house's hold over her. But the whispers grew louder, filling her mind with a cold, suffocating darkness that made it hard to breathe, hard to think.

In a final, desperate act, Mara opened her eyes, her gaze locking onto the mirror across the room. She saw her reflection, pale and frightened, but she also saw something else—a faint glimmer, a spark of light that seemed to flicker within the shadows.

It was a reflection of herself, yet different. Stronger. Determined.

With a surge of will, she reached out to her reflection, her voice filled with a fierce resolve. "I will not stay. You will not take me."

The house seemed to shudder, the shadows recoiling slightly, as though surprised by her defiance. The whispers grew softer, hesitant, as if the house itself were unsure, as if it hadn't anticipated resistance.

Seizing the moment, Mara pushed against the darkness that held her, her spirit flaring with a strength she hadn't known she possessed. She felt the shadows loosen, the air clearing slightly, and she moved toward the door, her steps firm, her heart filled with a fierce determination.

"I release you," she whispered, her voice filled with a quiet power, "and I release myself. Blackwood Manor will not have me."

The house groaned, the walls seeming to contract and expand, as if the very foundation were fighting against her words. But Mara held her ground, her spirit unwavering, her mind filled with the faces of those she had freed, the souls who had found peace at last.

And as the shadows retreated, as the whispers faded, she felt the grip of Blackwood Manor weaken, its hold slipping, as though the house itself were reluctantly letting go.

With a final, determined step, she reached the door, her hand pressing against the handle. This time, it moved, and she opened the door, stepping out into the cold, crisp air beyond, the house's presence falling away like a dark, suffocating veil.

As she crossed the threshold, she turned back, her gaze lingering on the manor's silent, shadowed facade. She could feel it watching her, its emptiness now complete, its hunger left unsatisfied. But it had released her, allowed her to leave, a reluctant surrender that left her shaken but free.

The house stood silent, its secrets buried within, its shadows waiting, watching.

And as Mara walked away, leaving Blackwood Manor behind, she knew she had won, but she also knew that the house would wait—for someone else, someone new, another lost soul to lure into its depths.

But Mara was free, and as she left the grounds, she felt a peace settle over her, a lightness that she hadn't felt since she first entered those haunted halls. She had freed the spirits, broken the curse, and, at last, escaped the clutches of Blackwood Manor.

But as she looked back one final time, she couldn't shake the feeling that the house was waiting, patient and silent, for its next visitor.

Chapter 22: Haunting Apparitions

Days passed, yet Mara couldn't shake the lingering presence of Blackwood Manor. Though she had escaped, her dreams remained haunted by images of the house—its dark corridors, its silent rooms, and, most vividly, Seraphina's pleading eyes. She told herself that she was free, that she had broken the curse, yet she felt an inexplicable pull drawing her back to the manor, as if some unfinished business lingered within its walls.

One night, as the wind howled outside her small cottage, Mara woke with a start, her heart racing, her mind filled with a single, undeniable urge: she had to return to Blackwood Manor. Something—perhaps Seraphina herself—was calling her back, and she knew that ignoring it would only deepen the feeling of unease that had settled within her.

As dawn broke, she found herself once again standing before the grand, decaying facade of Blackwood Manor. The house loomed in the early morning light, its shadow stretching across the overgrown lawn, silent yet alive with a palpable, oppressive energy. Taking a deep breath, Mara crossed the threshold, feeling the familiar chill settle over her as she stepped into the entryway.

The air inside was thick, almost electric, as if the house had been waiting for her return. She moved through the hallways, her footsteps echoing in the silence, and it wasn't long before she began to see them—the apparitions, vivid and almost painfully real.

In the grand salon, she saw Seraphina, her figure translucent but unmistakable, standing near the fireplace. Her dress was elegant but worn, her hair pinned back in the severe style Mara had seen in the portrait. But there was something different about her now—a sadness, yes, but also a fierce determination, an energy that seemed to pulse from her ghostly form.

As Mara watched, a second figure appeared—a man, tall and imposing, his face sharp with a cruel edge. He moved toward Seraphina, his eyes cold and unreadable, his movements filled with a harsh, calculated intent. Mara recognized him immediately. It was Henry, Seraphina's husband, the man who had betrayed her, whose infidelity had shattered her heart and driven her to madness.

Seraphina's face twisted with a mix of love and bitterness as she reached out to him, her hand hovering just shy of his arm, a sorrowful longing etched across her face. But before she could touch him, a shadowy figure slipped into the room—a woman with dark, flowing hair, her face turned away, her expression hidden.

Henry moved toward the woman, his posture softening, a faint smile playing on his lips. Seraphina watched, her gaze filled with a rage that seemed to flicker like flames, her ghostly form trembling as the memory replayed before Mara's eyes.

Suddenly, the room filled with voices, layered whispers that echoed from all directions, blending together in a chaotic symphony of anger, betrayal, and sorrow. Mara clutched her arms, feeling the weight of the emotions pressing down on her, filling the space around her.

"You betrayed me," Seraphina's voice hissed, her words laced with venom. "You promised me your love, your loyalty, yet you turned to her, leaving me to suffer in silence."

Henry's figure turned, his face twisting with anger, his voice cold and dismissive. "Your love was a prison, Seraphina. You clung to me, bound me to your grief, your madness. I had to escape—to find freedom."

The woman beside him stepped forward, her figure more defined now, her face visible. Mara recognized her as well—she was a family friend, someone Seraphina had trusted, had welcomed into her home, never suspecting the betrayal that would come.

Seraphina's expression darkened, her form growing more solid, more intense, her sorrow giving way to a fury that pulsed through the room, filling every corner, every shadow. Mara could feel it pressing against her, suffocating in its intensity, a rage so consuming it seemed to burn through the air.

"I gave you everything," Seraphina's voice echoed, each word a dagger laced with bitterness. "And for that, you condemned me. You turned me into a ghost, a shell of the woman I once was."

The scene shifted suddenly, and Mara found herself in the dining room, where another apparition played out before her. Seraphina stood at the head of the table, her eyes wide with disbelief as Henry laughed with his supposed lover, their flirtation open, cruelly blatant. The room filled with murmurs, the faint, ghostly echoes of the other guests, their expressions shifting between discomfort and amusement, their eyes casting judgment on Seraphina as she watched, helpless, humiliated.

Mara's heart ached as she watched Seraphina relive these moments, trapped in a loop of betrayal and despair. She wanted to reach out, to comfort her, but she knew that these were only echoes, memories replaying endlessly, fragments of a past that Seraphina couldn't escape.

As she moved through the house, Mara saw more apparitions—ghostly figures moving through the halls, their forms flickering and fading like shadows cast by candlelight. She saw Seraphina in her bedroom, weeping as she clutched the locket that held her child's portrait, whispering words of love and desperation to a figure only she could see.

In the attic, Mara witnessed the widow standing alone, surrounded by candles, her hands trembling as she chanted, her voice filled with an intense, unyielding desire. She watched as Seraphina performed the rituals, her movements frantic, her face pale and hollowed, her eyes filled with a madness that had been born from betrayal and loss.

Each room seemed to hold a new vision, each one more vivid than the last, and Mara felt herself slipping deeper into the house's memories, the line between past and present blurring, merging into a seamless, haunting tapestry of sorrow and resentment.

Finally, she found herself back in the grand salon, where Seraphina's ghostly figure stood, her expression calm yet filled with a deep, unending sadness. She looked at Mara, her gaze piercing, as though she could see directly into her soul.

"Do you understand now?" Seraphina's voice was soft, almost gentle, but there was a darkness to it, a depth that made Mara's heart ache.

Mara nodded, her voice barely a whisper. "Yes, Seraphina. I see it all now. Your pain, your betrayal... the love that twisted into something darker."

Seraphina's gaze softened, her form flickering as if she were struggling to hold herself together. "I wanted them to suffer as I suffered," she said, her voice barely audible. "I wanted them to feel the weight of their betrayal, to be bound to this house as I was bound to my sorrow."

Mara felt a tear slip down her cheek, her empathy for Seraphina overwhelming. "You're free now," she whispered, her voice trembling. "You don't have to relive this anymore. Let go of the pain. Release yourself from this place."

Seraphina's form began to fade, her expression one of relief mixed with sadness. "Thank you, Mara. For helping me see... for reminding me of what I truly wanted."

As Seraphina's figure dissolved into mist, Mara felt a final, soft whisper drift through the room, filled with a peace that had eluded the widow in life.

"Goodbye."

The house grew silent, the apparitions fading one by one, their voices quieting until only Mara remained, standing alone in the grand salon. The air felt lighter, the oppressive energy that had haunted Blackwood Manor lifting, leaving behind a stillness that was both peaceful and haunting.

With a deep breath, Mara made her way to the door. This time, as she turned the handle, it opened easily, the sunlight spilling into the house, filling the room with warmth.

She stepped outside, feeling the weight of the house fall away from her, replaced by a profound sense of closure. Blackwood Manor had finally released its hold on her, and on those who had been bound within its walls. She looked back one last time, her gaze lingering on the windows, now empty, silent.

The house stood as it always had, grand and shadowed, but there was a new stillness to it, a quiet that spoke of peace rather than torment.

With a final, silent farewell, Mara turned and walked away, leaving Blackwood Manor and its ghosts behind, knowing that its story had finally come to an end.

Chapter 23: The Portrait's Smile

Though Mara had left Blackwood Manor behind, her mind was still haunted by visions of the house and its tragic inhabitants. She thought she had found closure, yet something continued to gnaw at her, a lingering unease that wouldn't let go. Every night, as she lay in bed, she could feel the presence of the house, a dark shadow at the edge of her consciousness, pulling her back toward its secrets.

One evening, feeling overwhelmed by the persistent memories, Mara once again returned to Blackwood Manor, hoping to finally confront whatever remnants lingered within its walls. This time, the house greeted her with an almost welcoming silence, as if it had been expecting her return.

As she made her way through the familiar halls, her eyes were drawn to the large, imposing portrait of Seraphina that hung in the main corridor. She had passed it countless times, but tonight, something about it seemed different—strange, almost alive. The widow's dark eyes seemed to follow her every movement, a shadowed intensity in them that made Mara shiver.

She stepped closer, her gaze locked on Seraphina's face. The portrait had always depicted the widow with a solemn expression, her features set in a sorrowful yet dignified mask. But tonight, as Mara looked, she could swear she saw something different—a hint of a smile, dark and knowing, tugging at the corners of Seraphina's lips.

A chill ran down Mara's spine, and she stepped back, her heart pounding. The expression was subtle, almost imperceptible, yet it filled her with a sense of dread that was both irrational and overwhelming. The widow's eyes seemed to gleam with a cruel amusement, as if she were watching Mara's every thought, her every emotion, and finding some twisted satisfaction in it.

"Seraphina..." Mara whispered, barely able to form the words. "What do you want?"

The room remained silent, the shadows pooling around her, yet she felt as if the house were listening, as if Seraphina herself were lingering, a silent presence woven into the very fabric of Blackwood Manor.

As she stared at the portrait, the smile grew more pronounced, transforming Seraphina's once sorrowful face into something mocking, sinister. Her dark eyes sparkled with a cunning glint, a hint of satisfaction that made Mara's skin crawl.

A sudden thought struck her, a possibility that filled her with horror. What if Seraphina's spirit had not left? What if, in freeing the others, Mara had inadvertently strengthened Seraphina's hold on the house, amplifying her presence, leaving her spirit alone and unchecked?

"No," Mara whispered, her voice trembling. "I did everything right. I freed you all. You're supposed to be at peace."

But the portrait seemed to disagree. The smile widened, stretching into something grotesque, a twisted mask of satisfaction and malice. Mara felt a strange pressure in her chest, a heaviness that made it difficult to breathe, as if the house itself were pressing down on her, feeding off her despair.

"Why are you still here?" she asked, her voice barely above a whisper. "What do you want from me?"

A faint whisper echoed through the room, so soft she could barely make it out, yet filled with a venom that made her blood run cold.

"You cannot free what does not wish to be freed..."

The words hung in the air, lingering like smoke, filling her mind with a sinking dread. She realized, with a chill, that Seraphina hadn't wanted peace. Her spirit had thrived on the sorrow, the anger, the endless cycle of betrayal and bitterness that had bound her to Blackwood Manor. And now, with the other spirits gone, Seraphina's presence had intensified, her influence spreading like a dark shadow, filling the house with her silent, consuming despair.

Mara stumbled back, her gaze still locked on the portrait as Seraphina's smile widened further, her eyes filled with a dark, twisted satisfaction. The widow's spirit hadn't been trapped by the curse alone—she had become one with the house, her essence woven into its walls, thriving off the despair that lingered within its halls.

Desperation filled Mara as she realized the truth. Seraphina had allowed herself to be "freed" from her human sorrow, but her spirit had become something else, something darker, something that fed off the pain of others.

"You want me to stay," Mara murmured, the words sinking in with a heavy finality. "You want me to be trapped here, like them."

The portrait seemed to pulse with a dark energy, Seraphina's eyes narrowing with a sinister glee. Mara could feel the house closing in around her, the walls seeming to shift and bend, the shadows growing thicker, more oppressive.

In a moment of panic, she turned and fled, her footsteps echoing through the hallways as she raced toward the exit. But as she reached the door, it refused to open, the handle stuck fast, as though the house itself were holding her in place.

Desperate, she ran through the corridors, searching for another way out, but every door, every window, was barred, locked, unyielding. The house had become a prison, its shadows deepening, thickening, as if feeding off her fear, her growing despair.

Behind her, she heard the faint sound of laughter, a soft, mocking echo that seemed to drift from the walls themselves, filling the air with a dark, twisted joy. It was Seraphina's voice, blending with the whispers of the house, as if she had become its very essence, a living shadow that lingered in every corner, every wall.

Exhausted, Mara stumbled into the grand salon, her breath coming in ragged gasps, her heart pounding with a terror she couldn't contain. She looked around, her eyes scanning the empty room, her mind racing as she tried to find a way out, a way to escape the house's grasp.

The walls seemed to pulse with a dark energy, and in the mirror across the room, Mara saw her reflection—pale, wide-eyed, her expression filled with a despair that mirrored Seraphina's, her own face twisted with the same bitterness and rage that had consumed the widow.

She realized, with a chilling clarity, that Seraphina's spirit had seeped into her, filling her with the same sorrow, the same resentment that had bound the widow to the house. The curse had lifted, but the house's hunger had not been satisfied—it had simply shifted its focus, its grasp now extending to her.

Mara sank to her knees, feeling the weight of the house pressing down on her, her spirit weakening, her own despair feeding into the shadows that surrounded her. The laughter grew louder, filling her mind, her heart, until she could barely think, barely breathe.

As she knelt there, her gaze drifted back to the portrait, where Seraphina's smile had transformed into a full, triumphant grin, her eyes gleaming with a dark satisfaction.

"You are mine now," the whisper filled her mind, a final, chilling confirmation of what she had feared.

Mara felt the last of her resolve crumble, the shadows pulling her deeper into their embrace, her spirit fading, merging with the darkness that filled Blackwood Manor.

And as her vision dimmed, the last thing she saw was Seraphina's smile, the triumphant, twisted grin of a spirit who had won, who had claimed another soul to add to her collection.

Blackwood Manor was hers once more, and it would continue to wait, patient and hungry, for the next soul brave—or foolish—enough to step through its doors.

Chapter 24: The Attic Ritual

Mara's nerves were raw, her heart heavy with the knowledge of what she had uncovered. Blackwood Manor had always been haunted, but her recent discoveries revealed something more sinister than restless spirits: the house itself seemed to feed off sorrow and despair, holding souls captive in a dark web woven by Seraphina's final curse. And now, Mara sensed that something in the manor wasn't finished with her—that the house, or whatever resided within it, had designs on her spirit, too.

Driven by a compulsion she couldn't resist, Mara found herself ascending the narrow staircase to the attic, the steps creaking underfoot, each one echoing through the silence. The air grew colder as she climbed, thick with dust and the smell of decay. She shivered, clutching her arms tightly around herself, yet unable to turn back. Something had been left for her in the attic, and it was time to confront it.

At the top of the stairs, she found herself in a dim, shadowed space. The walls and floor were covered with dust, the air heavy and stale. The objects scattered around the attic seemed frozen in time: antique trunks, cracked furniture draped in thick sheets, and boxes overflowing with forgotten relics. But as her eyes adjusted to the darkness, something else caught her attention—a faint, flickering glow in the far corner of the room.

Mara moved toward the light, her heart pounding as she drew closer. The glow was coming from a series of candles arranged in a circle, their flames casting eerie shadows that danced along the walls. In the center of the circle lay a series of strange symbols drawn in dark, dried liquid—likely blood—forming intricate shapes and sigils that pulsed faintly with a dark energy. It was as if the remnants of the ritual still held some semblance of power, an energy that hung in the air like a thick fog.

As she knelt to inspect the symbols, Mara felt a shiver run through her. The symbols were familiar, similar to those she had seen in Seraphina's journals and the secret room, markings meant to bind, to trap. Her mind reeled as she pieced together the intention behind this ritual. It was designed to do more than just summon; it was crafted to bind souls to the house, to ensnare them within its walls for eternity, feeding the darkness that had taken root within Blackwood Manor.

Realization struck her like a blow. This was the ritual Seraphina had used to create the curse, the very act that had bound her husband, her betrayers, and eventually herself, to the manor. And now, standing in the center of the ritual circle, Mara felt a chill settle over her—a cold certainty that this curse was meant for her as well.

A faint whisper echoed through the attic, soft and chilling, a voice filled with longing and resentment.

"You are here, as I was... alone, betrayed. You understand, don't you?"

Mara froze, her breath catching in her throat. The voice was unmistakably Seraphina's, filled with a hollow, desperate bitterness that seemed to seep into the very walls.

"No," Mara whispered, her voice trembling. "I don't belong here. I came to free you, to release the others."

But the whisper grew louder, wrapping around her like a dark embrace, filling the space with a sense of inevitability.

"You think you can escape? That you can leave, after all you have seen? The house has taken you, as it took me. It needs you, as it needed me."

The air around Mara grew colder, the shadows thickening, closing in. She looked around frantically, her gaze falling on the remnants of the ritual, the symbols seeming to pulse with a dark energy, feeding off her fear. She felt an invisible force pressing down on her, binding her, rooting her to the spot, as though the house itself had claimed her as its own.

"No," she said, her voice firmer this time. "I won't be another victim. I won't let you keep me here."

But even as she spoke, the shadows coiled tighter, pressing down on her, filling her with a cold, suffocating despair. Images flashed through her mind—visions of herself wandering the halls, trapped in an endless loop of sorrow, her spirit feeding the darkness of Blackwood Manor. She saw herself bound to the house, another lost soul caught in its web, reliving her fears and regrets, her life fading into the shadows.

Desperation welled within her, and she looked around, her eyes landing on a small, rusted dagger lying beside the circle of candles. She reached for it, her hand trembling, clutching it tightly as she tried to steady herself. The dagger was simple, its blade tarnished with age, yet she felt a faint pulse of energy emanating from it, a glimmer of hope amidst the darkness.

"You cannot fight it," the voice whispered, growing softer, almost tender. "Accept your place. The house will give you purpose, as it did for me."

Mara gripped the dagger tighter, her resolve hardening. She knew, with a bone-deep certainty, that this was her only chance. The ritual, the symbols—these were the tools that had trapped Seraphina and the others, but perhaps, in destroying them, she could break the house's hold over her.

Taking a steadying breath, she raised the dagger and began to scratch over the symbols, disrupting their intricate shapes, her movements hurried and desperate. Each stroke seemed to weaken the energy around her, the shadows retreating slightly, as though the house were fighting to hold on to her.

As she carved through the last symbol, a surge of energy exploded outward, a shockwave that filled the room with a blinding light. The shadows screamed, a shrill, piercing sound that echoed through the attic, filling her with a mixture of terror and triumph.

The light faded, and Mara collapsed to her knees, gasping for breath. The attic was silent, the candles extinguished, the symbols broken, their power severed. She felt a strange lightness, as though a weight had lifted from her, the house's dark presence receding, leaving behind only an echo of its former hold.

But as she rose, a final whisper filled the room, faint and hollow, laced with a sadness that seemed to linger, even in defeat.

"You are free... but the house will remember."

Mara shivered, the words chilling her to the core. She knew that Blackwood Manor would not simply let go, that its darkness would remain, waiting, watching, biding its time. But for now, she was free.

She left the attic, descending the stairs with a sense of finality, her steps steady and resolute. The house was quiet, the oppressive energy that had filled its halls finally gone, leaving behind a strange, almost peaceful silence.

As she crossed the threshold and stepped into the morning light, Mara felt the last remnants of Blackwood Manor's hold slip away, replaced by a profound sense of relief.

Yet, as she walked away, she couldn't shake the feeling that the house was watching her, that its shadowed windows held a quiet, waiting presence—a reminder that Blackwood Manor's darkness was not gone, only dormant, and that one day, it might find another soul to claim.

But Mara had escaped, and as she looked back one final time, she felt a fierce, defiant strength rise within her. She had broken the ritual, severed the ties, and freed herself from the house's grasp.

And though she knew the darkness of Blackwood Manor would live on, waiting patiently for the next lost soul, Mara had reclaimed her own.

Chapter 25: The Widow's Voice

Mara had thought she was free.

Since her escape from Blackwood Manor, she had been haunted by shadows, faint memories, and echoes of voices that seemed to linger just beyond hearing. But she had pushed them aside, focusing on the simple tasks of daily life, grounding herself in reality, reminding herself that the house's influence was behind her.

But the voice began again, soft at first, barely a whisper. It slipped into her thoughts in the dead of night, a faint murmur that grew louder, more insistent with each passing day.

"They betrayed me. They must pay."

The voice was unmistakably Seraphina's—cold, vengeful, and filled with a bitterness that made Mara's skin prickle. She tried to shake it off, reminding herself that she had broken the curse, destroyed the ritual, severed the ties that bound her to Blackwood Manor. But the voice persisted, slipping into her mind when she was least expecting it, a dark undercurrent that tugged at her thoughts, urging her to remember, to act.

The first night she heard it, Mara had bolted upright in bed, her heart pounding as the whispered words echoed through her mind. She searched her room, convinced she'd find a trace of the house's darkness lingering, but everything was as it should be—quiet, empty, untouched.

Still, she couldn't shake the feeling that something had followed her, a fragment of Blackwood Manor's presence, lingering like a dark shadow at the edges of her consciousness.

"Finish it," the voice whispered one evening, its tone colder, more demanding. "They deserve to suffer, as I have suffered."

Mara pressed her hands over her ears, as if blocking the sound physically could keep it out. "Leave me alone," she whispered, her voice trembling. "I freed you. I released your spirit. You're supposed to be gone."

But Seraphina's voice only grew stronger, filling the room with a chilling intensity. "You cannot release what doesn't wish to be freed. I am part of you now, Mara. You understand me. You felt my pain."

Mara's breath came in shallow gasps, her mind racing with images of the betrayal, the bitterness, the endless torment that had defined Seraphina's life. It was as if, in attempting to sever the house's hold, she had instead absorbed some fragment of Seraphina's rage, an indelible mark that lingered within her, refusing to let go.

The days that followed were a blur, Mara's mind filled with whispers and flashes of memory that were not her own. She saw images of Henry's cold smile, the look of betrayal in his eyes as he turned to another woman, the cruel, mocking glances of the guests who had witnessed Seraphina's humiliation. Each memory stirred a dark resentment within her, a bitterness she hadn't known she was capable of.

She fought against it, reminding herself that these were not her memories, not her emotions. But the voice persisted, blending her thoughts with Seraphina's, urging her to act, to finish the revenge that the widow had begun so long ago.

"They deserve to suffer," the voice hissed, filling her mind with a cold fury. "They took everything from me. Now you must take everything from them."

Mara found herself slipping, her own thoughts blurring with the widow's, her mind clouded with images of vengeance and retribution. She became withdrawn, her focus consumed by the relentless whispering that haunted her every moment, growing louder, more insistent, until it drowned out everything else.

One night, as the whispering reached a fever pitch, Mara caught her reflection in the mirror and froze. Her face was pale, her eyes hollow, filled with a darkness she didn't recognize. And there, in her expression, was something disturbingly familiar—a bitterness, a twisted satisfaction, the very look she had seen on Seraphina's face in the portrait at Blackwood Manor.

The realization struck her like a cold wave. She was becoming Seraphina.

"No," Mara whispered, shaking her head, backing away from the mirror. "This isn't me. I won't let you do this to me."

The voice laughed, a soft, mocking sound that filled the room with a chilling intensity. "You already have. You felt my pain, my betrayal. You know the darkness that lingers in the hearts of those who would betray love, loyalty."

Mara closed her eyes, her hands trembling. "I'm not like you, Seraphina. I won't let your bitterness consume me."

But the voice continued, relentless, weaving its way through her mind, each word pressing deeper, planting seeds of resentment, memories of betrayal. "They will betray you too, Mara. They always do. Finish what I could not. Make them suffer as I have suffered."

Mara felt a dark anger rising within her, a cold resentment that was both foreign and disturbingly familiar. The memories of Seraphina's betrayal seemed to merge with her own insecurities, her fears, each one amplified by the widow's voice, filling her with a growing sense of vengeance.

She gripped the edges of the dresser, her knuckles white as she fought against the pull, her own voice a desperate whisper. "No, Seraphina. I won't give in to your bitterness. I released you—I freed your spirit. This is over."

But the voice only laughed again, a hollow, bitter sound that echoed through the room, filling her with a sense of dread that seemed to seep into her very bones.

"You can never be free. Not from me."

Mara felt tears prick at her eyes, a cold terror settling over her as she realized the extent of Seraphina's hold. The widow's spirit had indeed been released from Blackwood Manor, but it had not left Mara. Instead, it had taken root within her, embedding itself in her mind, her thoughts, like a dark parasite that fed on her fears, her anger, her pain.

She sank to the floor, her body shaking as she fought against the darkness that threatened to consume her. She knew, with a sickening certainty, that Seraphina's vengeance was not over—that, somehow, the widow's spirit had latched onto her, binding her to the curse, urging her to finish what Seraphina had started.

For days, Mara isolated herself, wrestling with the voice, trying to drown out the whispers that filled her mind. She tried everything—meditation, distraction, even leaving the town in an attempt to escape the reach of Blackwood Manor's influence. But the voice followed her, relentless, growing louder, more insistent, filling her with an unshakeable need for vengeance, a hunger that seemed to grow with each passing moment.

And as she stood one night, staring into the mirror, her own face twisted with a bitterness that wasn't entirely her own, Mara realized that Seraphina's curse was far from over.

Blackwood Manor had claimed her, and now, she was part of its dark legacy, a vessel for the widow's vengeance, a new host for the curse that would continue to feed on the sorrow, the bitterness, and the despair of those who dared to seek its secrets.

The widow's voice echoed in her mind, a final, chilling whisper that filled her with a dread that she knew would never leave.

"You are mine, Mara. You always have been."

And as the voice faded, leaving only a cold silence in its wake, Mara knew that she would never truly be free—that Blackwood Manor's darkness had taken root within her, a shadow that would follow her wherever she went, a curse that would linger, silent and insidious, waiting for the moment it could rise again.

Chapter 26: Lost in Time

Mara had tried everything to escape Seraphina's voice, yet the widow's presence clung to her like a shadow, darkening her thoughts, consuming her spirit. She was no longer certain where her own emotions ended and Seraphina's began. The boundaries between past and present blurred until they felt like two sides of the same coin, each feeding into the other, a relentless cycle of sorrow and vengeance.

It started subtly, with brief flashes—a glimpse of a room as it had once been, filled with rich furnishings and flickering candlelight, or a fleeting memory of faces she didn't know but felt she'd met before. She would find herself walking down the hallways, only to feel the walls around her shift, morphing into the opulent decor of a time long past. She tried to shake it off, telling herself they were just remnants of Blackwood Manor's influence, echoes of her time spent there. But the sensations grew stronger, lasting longer, until she began to feel as though she were slipping into another reality altogether.

One afternoon, as she was walking to her kitchen, she felt a strange pull, an invisible tug that drew her back toward the front door. She tried to resist, her mind screaming that she didn't want to go back to Blackwood Manor, but her feet moved of their own accord, each step an echo of a life she didn't recognize but couldn't ignore. Her vision blurred, and suddenly, she wasn't in her cottage at all.

She was back in Blackwood Manor, standing in the grand salon, the room darkened by thick, velvet curtains that cast heavy shadows over the walls. The furniture was pristine, untouched by time, and the air was filled with the faint scent of lavender and wax, a mixture she had come to associate with the widow. She looked down at her hands and gasped—her fingers were adorned with delicate rings, each one glinting in the dim candlelight, her skin pale and smooth.

She was no longer herself. She was Seraphina.

Panic welled within her, but her body moved without her control, her hands trailing along the edges of a table as she walked slowly through the room. She could feel Seraphina's thoughts weaving into her own, a sorrow so deep it seemed to seep into her bones. Each step was filled with an eerie familiarity, as though she had walked this path a thousand times, always ending in despair.

"They betrayed me," her voice whispered, a soft, hollow sound that echoed through the room, tinged with both bitterness and resignation. She knew, instinctively, that this was Seraphina's final night—the night she had sealed her fate, casting the curse that would bind her, and others, to Blackwood Manor forever.

Mara felt herself drawn toward the grand staircase, her steps slow and deliberate. She ascended the stairs, each one creaking beneath her, the sound like an echo of her own fractured memories. She felt trapped in Seraphina's mind, her own thoughts swallowed by the widow's emotions, her vision a haze of sorrow and rage.

As she reached the top of the staircase, she turned toward the east wing, her feet carrying her to the room that had once been her sanctuary. She entered, feeling the cold, empty silence that filled the space, a stark contrast to the warmth it had once held. The furniture was draped in shadows, the mirror reflecting a ghostly image that looked both like herself and like Seraphina, their faces merging, blending, until she couldn't tell where one ended and the other began.

The room grew colder, and Mara felt Seraphina's emotions intensify, a torrent of bitterness and betrayal that filled her mind with a dark clarity.

"They deserve to suffer, as I have suffered."

The voice was hers, yet not hers, a thought that was both familiar and foreign, filling her with a resolve that frightened her. She knew that Seraphina had taken these steps before, had stood in this room, her mind consumed by a desire for vengeance, her heart hollowed by betrayal. And now, as Mara relived those moments, she felt the same darkness creeping into her soul, a cold whisper that urged her to surrender, to accept her place within Blackwood Manor's curse.

She closed her eyes, willing herself to break free, to resist the pull of Seraphina's memories. But when she opened them again, she was no longer in the east wing. She was in the attic, standing in the center of a ritual circle, the symbols on the floor glowing faintly, as though pulsing with a life of their own.

Her vision blurred, and she saw Seraphina's final act—the pouring of the dark liquid, the lighting of the candle, the chanting of the curse that would bind souls to the house, trapping them in a cycle of despair. She felt Seraphina's anger, her need to make those who had wronged her suffer, her desire to weave her pain into the very walls of the house, so that it would linger, unending, a prison for both the guilty and herself.

As the ritual reached its peak, Mara felt her own spirit merging with Seraphina's, her thoughts filled with a darkness that wasn't entirely her own. She saw flashes of her own life, her own moments of betrayal and pain, each one amplifying Seraphina's rage, blending their sorrows into a single, consuming force.

"It is your turn now," Seraphina's voice whispered, filled with a cold satisfaction. "You know the pain of betrayal, of loss. Finish what I began."

Mara felt the weight of Seraphina's expectations pressing down on her, an unyielding force that threatened to consume her entirely. She realized, with a growing sense of horror, that the widow's curse was not simply a trap for others; it was a legacy, passed down to those who could understand, who could feel the depth of Seraphina's sorrow and carry it forward.

"No," Mara whispered, her voice trembling. "I won't be part of this. I won't let you take me."

But the attic grew darker, the shadows closing in around her, Seraphina's voice filling her mind, urging her to surrender, to give in to the cycle, to accept her place within the house's twisted history.

"You have already taken my place," Seraphina's voice whispered, a cruel edge in her tone. "The house has chosen you, Mara. You cannot escape."

Mara felt a cold despair settle over her as the room spun, her vision blurring until she was no longer in the attic but back in the grand salon, her face reflected in the large mirror above the fireplace. She saw Seraphina's expression staring back at her, a bitter smile twisting her lips, her eyes filled with a dark satisfaction that made Mara's blood run cold.

She reached out to the mirror, her hand trembling as she touched the glass, feeling the cold surface beneath her fingertips. She was trapped, lost in a loop of time and memory, unable to distinguish her own life from Seraphina's, her own desires from the widow's bitterness.

The reflection leaned closer, her voice a chilling whisper that seemed to echo through the room.

"You are me now, Mara. Embrace it. Relive it. Become the next chapter of Blackwood Manor."

As the reflection faded, Mara felt herself slipping further into the past, her own identity blurring as she walked through the house, reliving Seraphina's final night again and again, each moment sharpening, deepening, until she could no longer remember who she truly was.

Blackwood Manor had claimed her, its curse complete, the cycle renewed.

And Mara, lost in the echoes of the past, became the newest ghost in its unending story, bound to the house by the same sorrow, the same bitterness, reliving the widow's tragedy for eternity.

Chapter 27: The Caretaker's Confession

Mara was spiralling. Each day, the lines between her own life and Seraphina's grew thinner, her own memories mingling with the widow's anguish, her own desires replaced by the bitterness that had fuelled Seraphina's curse. The world outside Blackwood Manor felt distant, unreal, as though she were already lost in a fog that wrapped her deeper into the house's grip.

But one morning, as she wandered the empty hallways in a haze, she saw someone she hadn't expected to see: Mrs. Havers, the house's supposed caretaker, a figure Mara had only encountered occasionally and had long assumed was an ordinary caretaker overseeing the estate. Yet now, as she looked at Mrs. Havers with new eyes, Mara saw a weariness in her face, a heaviness that seemed to mirror her own.

The older woman was standing by a window in the east wing, her gaze fixed on something unseen, her posture stiff and rigid. Mara approached cautiously, her voice soft, almost hesitant.

"Mrs. Havers?"

The woman turned slowly, her eyes meeting Mara's with a mixture of sorrow and resignation. She didn't respond immediately, instead looking at Mara with an intensity that made her shiver.

"You know, don't you?" Mrs. Havers said at last, her voice low and tinged with a sadness that seemed to echo through the hallway.

Mara nodded, unsure of what to say, her heart heavy with the weight of the truth she had been unravelling piece by piece. "I know... I know that Seraphina's curse lingers here. I know that it's bound people to this house, including me."

Mrs. Havers sighed, a sound filled with weariness. She looked away, her gaze returning to the window, her eyes distant. "You're right about one thing, dear. This house... it doesn't let go easily. Once it has its hold on you, there's little chance of escaping."

Mara's breath caught in her throat. The words, though softly spoken, struck her with a force that left her feeling hollow, as though she had already lost her battle against the darkness that clung to Blackwood Manor.

"But you... you've been here for so long," Mara said, her voice trembling. "You're the caretaker. Surely you can leave?"

A faint, humourless smile crossed Mrs. Havers' face, a bitter twist that made her appear even older than her years. She shook her head slowly. "Caretaker... that's what they call me, yes. It's a useful title, makes people think I have a choice. But the truth is, Mara, I'm not a caretaker by choice. I am bound to this house, just as much as Seraphina was. Just as you are now."

Mara's heart pounded, her mind reeling with confusion. "Bound? But how? I thought—"

Mrs. Havers turned to face her fully, her expression one of resignation. "Years ago, I came here as a young woman, much like you. I was drawn to the house, to its mysteries, its secrets. But I was naive, Mara. I thought I could uncover those secrets, that I could somehow break the curse. But the house... it doesn't work that way. It pulls you in, it gets into your thoughts, and before you realize it, you're part of its web, bound by the very secrets you thought you could unravel."

Mara felt a chill settle over her, her mind racing as she processed Mrs. Havers' words. She thought of all the times she had seen the woman moving through the house, her quiet presence almost ghostly, always watching, always knowing. She had thought Mrs. Havers was simply a caretaker, an observer of Blackwood Manor's haunting legacy. But now she realized that Mrs. Havers was as much a prisoner as she was.

"So you've... you've been here all this time?" Mara asked, her voice barely a whisper. "Unable to leave?"

Mrs. Havers nodded, her eyes filling with a deep sadness. "I've tried, in the early years. Many times, I tried to leave. But each time, I would find myself drawn back, as though an invisible chain held me here, binding me to the house. It's as if Blackwood Manor becomes a part of you, embedding itself in your mind, your soul, until you can't tell where the house ends and you begin."

Mara shuddered, feeling the weight of Mrs. Havers' confession settle over her like a dark veil. She understood now why the woman had always seemed so reserved, so withdrawn. She had been living in a prison, trapped by a curse that had consumed her life, turning her into a guardian of Blackwood Manor's secrets, forever bound to its walls.

"But why?" Mara asked, her voice filled with desperation. "Why did the house choose you? Why does it hold people here?"

Mrs. Havers looked at her with a resigned expression, her eyes haunted. "The house doesn't choose, Mara. It simply... absorbs. It takes in those who resonate with its sorrow, its bitterness. People who have suffered, who carry their own shadows, find themselves drawn here, unable to resist the pull. And once you've given a piece of yourself to Blackwood Manor, it never lets go."

Mara felt a cold despair settle over her. She thought of all the times she had felt the house's presence, the way it seemed to draw her deeper, feeding off her emotions, her fears. She had thought she was free when she left, but now she realized that Blackwood Manor had already claimed her, that her attempts to escape were little more than illusions.

"Is there no way to break it?" Mara asked, her voice trembling. "No way to escape?"

Mrs. Havers shook her head, her expression filled with a quiet resignation. "I don't know. I've tried everything I could think of. But the house's grip is strong, Mara, stronger than any curse, any ritual. It's as if the house itself is alive, feeding off the souls it holds, drawing strength from our sorrow."

Mara felt a tear slip down her cheek, the weight of Mrs. Havers' words filling her with a despair she couldn't shake. She realized now that her attempts to break Seraphina's curse had only scratched the surface, that the house's power was deeper, more insidious than she had ever imagined.

"So... I'm stuck here?" Mara whispered, her voice barely audible. "Like you?"

Mrs. Havers placed a gentle hand on Mara's shoulder, her gaze filled with empathy. "I'm afraid so, dear. But you're not alone. Blackwood Manor may hold us, but it doesn't mean we have to let it define us. There are ways to endure, ways to find peace, even within these walls."

Mara looked at her, a mixture of sorrow and gratitude filling her heart. She had thought of Mrs. Havers as merely a caretaker, a distant presence within the house, but now she saw her as something more—a kindred spirit, someone who understood the depths of Blackwood Manor's darkness, someone who shared her struggle.

"Thank you," Mara whispered, her voice thick with emotion. "I... I don't know if I can do this, but knowing you're here..."

Mrs. Havers smiled faintly, a glimmer of warmth in her weary eyes. "You're stronger than you know, Mara. The house may hold us, but it cannot take away our spirit. Remember that."

Mara nodded, a faint spark of hope igniting within her. She didn't know how she would survive, how she would endure the weight of Blackwood Manor's curse. But with Mrs. Havers by her side, a quiet but unwavering presence within the darkness, she felt a glimmer of strength.

As they stood together in the dim hallway, bound by the house's curse yet united in their defiance, Mara realized that she was not alone—and that perhaps, within the shadows of Blackwood Manor, there was still a sliver of light, a chance for resilience, for survival, even amidst the darkest of curses.

Part IV: Breaking the Web
Chapter 28: The Widow's Last Letter

The realization of her fate weighed heavily on Mara in the days that followed Mrs. Havers' confession. She was bound to Blackwood Manor, trapped in its web of sorrow and darkness, with only the faintest hope of ever escaping its grasp. Yet, there was something about Mrs. Havers' quiet strength, her resilience in the face of the curse, that gave Mara a reason to keep searching, to keep hoping.

It was during one of these solitary days, as she wandered the manor's halls, that Mara felt a strange pull toward Seraphina's private study—a room she had seldom entered, a place that seemed to hold an air of finality, as if the last remnants of the widow's spirit lingered there, waiting.

The study was dimly lit, the curtains drawn tightly over the windows, casting long shadows across the room. Dust hung in the air, thick and undisturbed, settling over the antique furniture and the shelves filled with old, forgotten books. Mara moved carefully, her fingers trailing along the dark wood of the desk, feeling the weight of Seraphina's presence. She could almost imagine the widow sitting there, her mind heavy with bitterness and regret.

As she traced the edges of the desk, her fingers brushed against something unusual—a faint seam beneath the wood, barely noticeable, as if it had been hidden deliberately. Her curiosity piqued, Mara pressed gently, and with a soft click, a hidden drawer slid open, revealing a single, yellowed envelope within.

Her breath caught as she reached for it, her fingers trembling. The envelope was addressed to Henry Blackwood, but it was clear from the faded ink and the age of the paper that it had never been sent. Mara carefully opened it, the brittle paper crackling as she unfolded the letter, her heart racing as she read Seraphina's final words.

My Dearest Henry,

I hardly know where to begin, or if these words will ever reach you. I write with a heart that is weary, with a soul that has suffered beneath the weight of betrayal, of love that has been twisted, broken by bitterness and sorrow. Perhaps you will never understand the depth of the pain I carry, but I must try, if only to free myself from it.

I have done things I never thought possible, things that haunt me as I write these words. In my darkest hours, I thought that binding you to this place would bring me peace, that seeing you suffer would somehow ease my own pain. But I was wrong. My heart is hollow, my spirit burdened by the very curse I placed upon you. It is as though I have bound myself, chained to these walls by my own bitterness, unable to escape the prison I created.

There are moments, Henry, fleeting as they are, when I long for freedom, for release from this endless cycle of sorrow and rage. I realize now that my actions have not only condemned you, but have condemned myself, trapping my soul in an unending loop of despair. I wanted revenge, yes, but I never considered the cost, the toll it would take on my own spirit.

I am weary, Henry. Weary of the darkness, of the hatred that has consumed me. There is a part of me that longs to forgive, to let go of the bitterness that binds me here. But I am afraid. Afraid of what lies beyond this place, afraid that there may be nothing left of me once the curse is lifted.

If, somehow, someone finds this letter, I hope they will understand that I was once more than the bitterness, more than the sorrow that now defines me. I was once a woman who loved deeply, who trusted foolishly, who gave everything for love.

To whoever finds this—if there is a way to free me, I beg you, release me from this curse. Allow me to find peace, to let go of the anger that binds me here. I am ready, at last, to be free.

In regret and sorrow,

Seraphina Blackwood

Mara's hands shook as she finished reading, tears slipping down her cheeks as the weight of Seraphina's words settled over her. She had always seen Seraphina as a figure consumed by bitterness and vengeance, a woman whose pain had led her to curse not only her betrayers but herself. Yet this letter revealed a side of the widow that Mara hadn't seen before—a soul broken by sorrow, a woman who had once loved deeply but had been left empty, hollowed by the very curse she had crafted.

The letter was more than just an apology; it was a plea, a desperate hope for redemption, for freedom from the darkness that had consumed her. Mara felt a surge of empathy, an understanding that went beyond words. She could feel Seraphina's regret, her longing for release, her desire to finally let go of the bitterness that had bound her to Blackwood Manor.

In that moment, Mara knew what she had to do. She had seen remnants of the ritual Seraphina had used to cast the curse in the attic, but perhaps, with this new knowledge, she could attempt something different—a ritual of release, one that would allow Seraphina to find peace and, perhaps, free herself in the process.

Clutching the letter, Mara made her way to the attic, the memory of Seraphina's final words burning in her mind. She reached the cold, shadowed space where the remnants of the binding ritual lay, the symbols faded but still faintly visible in the dust. Kneeling in the center of the ritual circle, she took a deep breath, her heart pounding as she prepared to begin.

She held the letter tightly, her voice soft but resolute as she spoke into the silence.

"Seraphina Blackwood, I have read your words. I understand your pain, your sorrow, your regret. I am here to release you from this curse, to free you from the bitterness that has bound you to this house. Let go of your anger, your desire for vengeance. Find peace."

The air around her grew colder, a faint, shimmering mist filling the room as if the house itself were listening, as though Seraphina's spirit were drawn by her words. The shadows seemed to shift, forming a ghostly figure in front of her—the faint outline of Seraphina, her face softened, her eyes filled with a sorrow that made Mara's heart ache.

"Seraphina," Mara whispered, holding up the letter. "I found your last words, your plea for freedom. I'm here to grant you that release. I'll finish this for you, I'll help you find peace."

The figure wavered, flickering as if caught between worlds, her gaze locked on Mara, a mixture of gratitude and regret in her eyes. The silence stretched between them, heavy and solemn, until, finally, Seraphina's voice echoed softly through the attic, a whisper filled with hope and sorrow.

"Thank you…"

Mara watched as Seraphina's figure began to fade, the shadows lifting, the weight of the curse loosening its grip. She could feel a lightness filling the room, a warmth that seeped into her bones, washing away the cold, oppressive energy that had lingered there for so long.

As Seraphina's spirit dissolved into the mist, Mara felt a tear slip down her cheek, her heart filled with a bittersweet relief. She had done it. She had freed the widow, released her from the cycle of bitterness and sorrow that had bound her to Blackwood Manor.

The attic grew silent, the shadows receding, leaving behind only an echo of peace, a stillness that filled the house with a sense of finality. Mara felt the weight lift from her own spirit as well, a release that left her feeling lighter, as though the darkness that had haunted her was finally gone.

As she descended the stairs, the letter still clutched in her hand, Mara felt a quiet strength settle within her. She had completed Seraphina's last wish, granted the widow the freedom she had longed for, and in doing so, she had freed herself.

And as she left Blackwood Manor for the final time, Mara knew that the house's dark legacy had come to an end.

Chapter 29: The Burial of Secrets

Though Mara had helped release Seraphina's spirit from the house, she still felt an unease lingering within Blackwood Manor. It was as if shadows remained, faint echoes of bitterness that clung to the walls, refusing to fade entirely. She realized that the curse, although weakened, was still not fully broken.

One morning, as she wandered the grounds, searching for answers, a strange thought occurred to her. Seraphina's final letter had spoken of regret and longing for peace, but there was something missing—a physical farewell, a place to lay her spirit fully to rest. She had released Seraphina's soul, but her memory, her secrets, might still be bound to something here on the estate, holding a part of her spirit tethered to the earth.

Determined to investigate further, Mara searched the grounds for any clue, any hidden sign that might lead her to what was left of Seraphina. Her steps took her toward the overgrown garden in the far corner of the estate, a place where few ventured, its pathways swallowed by thick vines and gnarled trees. The air here was heavier, the silence more profound, as though the garden held secrets long buried.

After hours of searching, she noticed a strange patch of ground near the edge of the garden, where the earth was slightly raised, a ring of withered flowers marking its perimeter. It looked like an unmarked grave, forgotten by time, hidden beneath layers of soil and neglect. Kneeling beside it, Mara brushed away the leaves and dirt, her hands trembling as she uncovered a faint outline of stone beneath the earth.

As she dug, her fingers scraped against something solid—a small, ornate box, its surface tarnished with age but unmistakably beautiful. She pulled it from the ground, her heart racing as she carefully opened the lid. Inside were personal belongings: a delicate brooch, a lock of hair bound with a black ribbon, a silver locket engraved with the initials S.B., and a small diary, its pages brittle with age.

These were Seraphina's belongings, keepsakes from her life before the curse, tokens of her love, her memories. It was clear now that someone—perhaps even Seraphina herself—had buried them here, attempting to hide away the remnants of a life she could never escape. Mara realized that these items, long interred and forgotten, might hold the final tether keeping Seraphina's memory bound to Blackwood Manor.

With a sense of reverence, Mara gathered the belongings and began to read the small diary, its pages filled with Seraphina's elegant handwriting. The entries were brief but poignant, speaking of love, loss, betrayal, and finally, a deep regret. It was as if Seraphina had poured her heart into these pages, her words filled with a raw vulnerability that left Mara feeling as though she were witnessing the widow's true, unguarded self.

One entry in particular caught her eye:

"I have bound myself to this place in bitterness and anger, yet my heart longs for release. If ever these words are found, if ever my keepsakes see the light of day once more, may they serve as a reminder of who I was, of the woman I loved, the life I cherished before it all went dark."

Mara felt a wave of empathy wash over her, the weight of Seraphina's sorrow pressing into her chest. This grave was more than a hiding place; it was a forgotten monument, a resting place for the memories Seraphina could not bear to carry with her into the afterlife. The curse, Mara realized, would never fully lift until Seraphina's memory was laid to rest—until her secrets, her life, were finally buried.

With a renewed sense of purpose, Mara decided to create a proper burial for Seraphina, to give her the peace she had sought but never found. She gathered what she needed—a small shovel, a cloth to wrap the belongings in—and chose a spot beneath the old oak tree, where the morning sun filtered through the branches, casting a soft, golden light over the ground.

She placed each item carefully in the earth: the brooch, the locket, the lock of hair, and finally, the diary, which she wrapped in the cloth as though tucking it into a bed. As she laid each item in the ground, she spoke softly, her words a farewell to the spirit who had suffered so long.

"Seraphina Blackwood," she whispered, her voice filled with compassion, "I release you from this place. I lay to rest your memories, your pain, and your sorrow. May you find peace now, away from the bitterness that bound you here. Your secrets are safe, buried with you, and remembered with love."

As she covered the belongings with soil, a breeze swept through the garden, rustling the leaves above her, carrying a faint, almost ethereal warmth. Mara felt a presence settle over her, a gentle, quiet peace that filled the air, as though Seraphina herself were watching, offering a final, silent gratitude.

When the burial was complete, Mara placed a small, wildflower bouquet atop the grave, the blooms vibrant and alive, a contrast to the sorrow that had once permeated the garden. She stood there for a long moment, her heart filled with a bittersweet relief, knowing that she had finally given Seraphina the rest she deserved.

As she turned to leave, the garden seemed brighter, the shadows retreating, replaced by a calm, almost sacred stillness. She felt the weight lift from her spirit, as though the house itself had exhaled, releasing the last remnants of darkness that had clung to it for so long.

Mara walked back to the manor, her steps light, her heart full of peace. She knew, without a doubt, that the curse had finally broken, that Seraphina's spirit had been laid to rest, her secrets buried, her memory honoured.

And as she left Blackwood Manor for the final time, Mara felt a quiet strength within her, a sense of closure that filled her with hope. The shadows of Blackwood Manor were gone, its halls empty, its story complete.

The house would stand silent, its secrets buried, its curse lifted.

And as Mara stepped out into the sunlight, she knew she was free.

Chapter 30: A Battle of Wills

Mara had thought she was free. She'd laid Seraphina's secrets to rest, buried the remnants of the widow's pain and regrets, and felt a peace settle over Blackwood Manor that hadn't been there before. But as she turned to leave the house one final time, a chill ran down her spine, a familiar, oppressive presence filling the air. The shadows lengthened, thickening around her, and the front door, which had stood open just moments ago, slammed shut with a resounding finality.

A soft, cold whisper filled the room, wrapping around her like a veil of ice.

"You think you can leave me, Mara?"

Mara froze, her heart pounding as the whisper turned into laughter, soft and mocking. It was Seraphina's voice, though it sounded darker, sharper, layered with an edge of desperation that sent chills through her bones. Mara clenched her fists, her resolve wavering as she faced the truth: Seraphina's spirit, despite the burial, hadn't fully let go.

"You're gone, Seraphina," Mara said, her voice trembling but resolute. "I released you. I laid your secrets to rest. You don't need to hold on to this place—or to me—any longer."

The air around her grew colder, the shadows thickening, twisting into faint, ghostly shapes that loomed at the edges of her vision. Seraphina's laughter echoed through the house, filled with bitterness and longing, an intensity that pulled at Mara, tempting her to stay.

"I was never truly at rest," Seraphina whispered, her voice a thread of sorrow. "You took away my pain, my regrets, but I am bound to this place by something deeper... by the very walls, the memories woven into every shadow. My spirit is Blackwood Manor, and it will not release me so easily."

Mara felt a heaviness settle over her, an invisible weight pressing down on her shoulders, filling her mind with Seraphina's memories, her despair, the sorrow that had transformed her into a creature of shadows, unable to let go.

"Then let go now, Seraphina," Mara said, struggling to keep her voice steady. "I've done everything I can. It's time for you to find peace."

But Seraphina's presence grew stronger, filling the room with an oppressive energy, a force that seemed to emanate from the walls themselves, binding Mara in place. The air grew colder, and Mara felt a strange, inexplicable longing rising within her, an urge to stay, to surrender, to let herself be a part of the manor's history, its legacy.

"You understand my pain, Mara," Seraphina's voice softened, almost pleading. "You know what it's like to be betrayed, to suffer in silence. You know the weight of loneliness, of regret. Stay with me. Don't leave me to this emptiness. Together, we could be stronger, bound by our sorrows, by our understanding. Blackwood Manor can be our sanctuary."

Mara closed her eyes, fighting against the wave of sorrow that filled her, the whispers that urged her to give in, to let herself be pulled into the house's darkness. The pull was powerful, familiar, and she felt herself weakening, her own memories mingling with Seraphina's, blurring until she could barely tell where she ended and the widow's spirit began.

But deep within her, a spark of defiance ignited, a fierce desire to survive, to resist the temptation that threatened to consume her. She thought of the life she had yet to live, the freedom she had fought so hard to reclaim, the sense of peace she had touched just moments ago. She wasn't ready to give that up—not for Seraphina, not for the house, not for the shadows that clung to her.

"No," she whispered, her voice filled with determination. "I won't stay, Seraphina. You can try to keep me, but I refuse to be bound here, trapped in your memories. I have my own life, my own story, and I won't let Blackwood Manor take it from me."

The shadows recoiled, as though wounded, and Seraphina's voice turned sharp, angry, the desperation in it giving way to fury.

"You cannot escape me, Mara. I am a part of you now, woven into your spirit. Even if you leave, you will carry my pain, my sorrow, everywhere you go. You will never truly be free."

Mara's resolve strengthened, her fear transforming into a fierce, unyielding strength. She had faced the darkness of Blackwood Manor, confronted Seraphina's pain, her regrets, and laid them to rest. The curse might have left echoes in her mind, memories that would linger, but they did not define her.

With a surge of courage, Mara took a step forward, her gaze unwavering as she faced the shadows. "You're wrong, Seraphina. I've given you the release you needed. I laid your secrets to rest, and I've seen the depths of your pain. But I am not yours to keep. I choose to leave this place, to live my life without the weight of your sorrow."

The air grew tense, charged with an electric energy as the shadows around her began to shift, swirling into a faint, ghostly form that resembled Seraphina, her face twisted with both rage and sorrow. Her ghostly eyes bore into Mara's, filled with an anguish that was both haunting and relentless.

"Then go, Mara," Seraphina whispered, her voice filled with bitterness, her form wavering as though caught between worlds. "But know this: the curse of Blackwood Manor is not easily forgotten. It will follow you, linger in the shadows of your memory, an echo that will haunt you always."

Mara felt a pang of fear, but she steadied herself, refusing to let Seraphina's words weaken her resolve. "If that is the price of freedom, I'll bear it. But I won't let your regrets, your sorrow, consume me any longer. Goodbye, Seraphina."

With those final words, Mara turned toward the door, her steps firm and unyielding. She felt the shadows claw at her, a last, desperate attempt to hold her back, to pull her into the house's dark embrace. But she pushed forward, her heart filled with a fierce, unbreakable will.

As she reached the door, she felt a cold breeze pass over her, a faint whisper that lingered in the air, filled with a bittersweet resignation.

"Goodbye, Mara..."

The door opened, and Mara stepped out into the morning light, the warmth of the sun flooding over her, washing away the last remnants of Blackwood Manor's hold. She felt a sense of release, a lightness that filled her soul, though she knew that a part of Seraphina's story would always remain with her, a shadow in the depths of her memory.

But as she walked away from Blackwood Manor for the final time, she felt a profound sense of peace. She had won the battle of wills, chosen her own path, and reclaimed her life. The house might linger in her thoughts, a faint echo of sorrow and darkness, but she was free.

And as she left the estate behind, the sun warming her face, Mara knew that the shadows of Blackwood Manor were finally at rest.

Chapter 31: Destroying the Portrait

Even after Mara's departure from Blackwood Manor, she felt its presence lingering, faint but undeniable. Seraphina's final whisper haunted her thoughts, an echo that seemed to cling to her like a shadow. As the days passed, Mara couldn't shake the feeling that the widow's spirit was still bound to the manor, held by some unseen tether that refused to release its grip.

Then she remembered the portrait.

The large, imposing painting of Seraphina had been a silent witness to all of Blackwood Manor's tragedies, its eyes following Mara wherever she went, filled with a bitterness that felt almost alive. She realized now that this portrait might be the last remnant holding Seraphina's spirit to the house. If the curse was to be fully broken, she would need to sever this final connection.

With a renewed determination, Mara returned to Blackwood Manor one last time, her steps firm as she crossed the threshold and headed straight for the grand hallway where the portrait hung. The air inside was colder than she remembered, thick with an eerie silence that pressed down on her, as if the house itself knew why she had returned.

The portrait loomed before her, its dark eyes filled with an unsettling intensity, watching her approach. Seraphina's expression, as always, was unreadable—an enigmatic mix of sorrow, anger, and something darker, something that felt almost predatory. The widow's gaze seemed to pierce through Mara, a silent challenge daring her to take this final step.

Mara took a deep breath, her heart racing as she reached for the matches she had brought with her. She struck one, the flame small but fierce, illuminating the shadowed hall in flickering light. Her gaze locked onto the portrait, and she felt Seraphina's presence grow stronger, filling the air with a thick, oppressive energy that seemed to pulse from the painting itself.

"Seraphina," Mara said, her voice steady. "This is the end. I'm releasing you from this house, breaking the last tether that keeps you here. You can't hold onto me—or this place—any longer."

As the flame danced in her hand, Mara saw the portrait's expression shift, almost imperceptibly. Seraphina's eyes narrowed, her lips curving into a faint, defiant smirk, as if she were daring Mara to go through with it, to face the consequences of destroying the only physical link left of the widow's legacy.

But Mara's resolve only strengthened. With a swift, deliberate motion, she touched the match to the bottom of the painting, watching as the flames caught onto the canvas, devouring the edge before spreading upward. The fire crackled, the heat building as it climbed, casting eerie shadows across the hallway as the portrait began to burn.

As the flames consumed Seraphina's image, a strange, piercing sound filled the air—a mix of a wail and a scream, as though the very spirit of the widow were crying out in anguish. The sound reverberated through the house, a final, desperate protest, filling Mara with a chill that made her skin prickle. She watched as the fire consumed Seraphina's face, the dark eyes staring out through the flames, filled with both rage and sorrow, a haunting reminder of the widow's pain and bitterness.

The scream grew louder, filling every corner of the house, and Mara felt the walls tremble, the floor vibrating beneath her feet as though the very foundation of Blackwood Manor was rebelling against this act, fighting to hold onto the last remnant of its curse. But Mara stood firm, her gaze unwavering as she watched the flames consume the painting, reducing Seraphina's image to ash.

As the fire reached the center of the portrait, the scream faded, replaced by a profound, almost deafening silence. The air grew still, the oppressive energy that had filled the house dissipating like smoke, leaving behind only an empty, hollow quiet. Mara felt a strange lightness settle over her, a release that filled her with a peace she hadn't felt since stepping into Blackwood Manor for the first time.

The portrait was gone, nothing left but charred remains and a faint wisp of smoke curling upward, vanishing into the shadows. Mara took a step back, her heart pounding as she let out a breath she hadn't realized she was holding. She could feel it—the curse had lifted, the final tether severed, the house finally free from Seraphina's sorrow and bitterness.

The walls seemed to relax, the oppressive weight gone, leaving only a quiet emptiness. Blackwood Manor, for the first time, felt like an ordinary house—no whispers, no shadows lurking in the corners, just silence.

As she turned to leave, Mara felt a faint, almost tender breeze brush past her, carrying with it the soft scent of lavender. It was as though Seraphina herself were offering a final farewell, a quiet, grateful acknowledgment of the release Mara had granted her.

Chapter 32: The House Crumbles

As the last remnants of Seraphina's portrait disintegrated into ash, an ominous rumble echoed through the hallway. The walls, once imposing and solid, began to tremble, fine cracks splintering along the surface like veins, spreading out from the charred remains of the portrait. Mara's eyes widened as she felt a deep, unsettling shift beneath her feet, the entire house seeming to shudder as though some ancient force within it had finally been released.

Blackwood Manor, once proud and grand, began to reveal its true, decayed form. The wallpaper peeled back in long, brittle strips, revealing rotting wood beneath. The ornate crown moulding crumbled, pieces falling to the floor in clouds of dust. The once-polished floors warped and splintered, creaking ominously under the weight of a past that could no longer be sustained.

Mara stumbled back, her hand instinctively covering her mouth as she watched the elegant facade of Blackwood Manor fall away, exposing the house's decay. Everything seemed to unravel in a twisted dance of destruction, as if the house were aging before her eyes, its timeless beauty eroding into ruin. It was as though Blackwood Manor had been holding itself together with Seraphina's curse, and now, with her spirit finally at peace, the illusion could no longer be maintained.

The chandeliers hanging above rattled violently, glass shards falling like rain, catching the dim light as they shattered against the floor. Dust filled the air, thick and suffocating, and Mara covered her mouth with her sleeve, her heart racing as she turned, her mind filled with a single thought: Get out.

She bolted down the hallway, feeling the ground give slightly beneath her with each step, the floorboards creaking and snapping like brittle bones. The walls around her groaned, the wood splintering, beams cracking under the weight of years of neglect and sorrow. Doors that had once stood firm now hung askew, their frames buckling, paint chipping away to reveal layers of decay beneath.

As she reached the grand staircase, she felt a surge of panic. The steps, once sturdy and majestic, now appeared warped and unstable, sagging under the weight of years suddenly unleashed. She took them two at a time, each step filling her with dread as the wood cracked beneath her feet. The banister, once carved with intricate details, crumbled beneath her grip, leaving her with nothing to hold onto but her determination to escape.

Reaching the bottom floor, she sprinted toward the main entryway, where the heavy front doors stood slightly ajar. She could see the sunlight streaming in, a stark contrast to the darkness consuming the manor behind her. But as she neared the door, a deafening crack sounded above, and Mara looked up just in time to see a section of the ceiling collapse, beams and debris crashing down mere inches from where she stood.

Dust and debris filled the air, and Mara coughed, her lungs burning as she pushed forward, her heart pounding with fear and adrenaline. The walls around her continued to buckle and split, peeling back to reveal layers of mold, damp rot, and crumbling plaster. The house, stripped of its pretence, was collapsing in on itself, its grandeur revealed to be nothing more than a façade held together by the bitterness of its haunting.

Mara's steps faltered as she neared the door, the floor beneath her groaning ominously, splintering as if threatening to give way entirely. She took one last look back, feeling a strange, bittersweet pang as she watched Blackwood Manor crumble around her, a relic of sorrow finally succumbing to time and decay.

"Goodbye, Seraphina," she whispered, a farewell to the spirit who had clung so fiercely to the house, a ghost whose pain had seeped into every wall, every corner, every shadow.

With a final burst of energy, Mara lunged toward the door, feeling the floor give way just as she threw herself across the threshold. She tumbled onto the front steps, gasping for breath, her body covered in dust, her heart pounding as she looked back.

Blackwood Manor stood silhouetted against the grey sky, its windows shattered, its walls crumbling, the entire structure buckling under the weight of its own history. The roof caved in with a thunderous crash, sending up a cloud of dust and debris, and the walls followed suit, collapsing inward like a house of cards. The once-grand mansion was reduced to rubble, a pile of stone and wood and memories buried beneath the weight of time.

As the dust settled, Mara felt a profound stillness, a sense of peace that she hadn't felt since she'd first set foot in the house. Blackwood Manor, with all its secrets, its sorrows, its ghostly memories, was gone. The curse, which had held the house and its spirits in a bitter grip, had finally been broken, taking the manor down with it.

Mara sat on the front steps, watching as the last remnants of Blackwood Manor settled into silence, the sun breaking through the clouds, casting a warm light over the ruins. She took a deep breath, feeling the weight of the past lift from her shoulders, her spirit light and free.

As she stood, she felt the faintest whisper on the breeze, a voice soft and almost indistinguishable, filled with gratitude and relief.

"Thank you."

Mara closed her eyes, a tear slipping down her cheek as she whispered a final farewell. The house was gone, its spirits at peace, its shadows finally laid to rest. And as she walked away, leaving the ruins behind, Mara knew that she, too, was free.

Chapter 33: The Final Goodbye

Days passed, and Mara slowly settled back into the quiet rhythm of her life, the memories of Blackwood Manor becoming a faint, distant echo. She had thought the house and its shadows were behind her, reduced to rubble, its curse broken and its spirits freed. Yet, as the sun set each night, she couldn't shake the feeling that a small part of the manor lingered, a subtle weight in the corners of her mind.

One evening, as she was organizing a few belongings she'd left packed during her time at Blackwood, Mara felt an odd sensation—a faint, tingling chill that settled over her as she opened a drawer in her dresser. Nestled beneath a few scattered papers was a delicate piece of lace, its edges frayed and worn. She froze, her breath catching in her throat as she realized what it was.

It was a small fragment of Seraphina's veil.

The lace was unmistakably familiar, with intricate, twisted patterns that seemed to mirror the sorrow and complexity of the widow's life. Mara ran her fingers over it, feeling a mix of emotions—fear, sadness, and an unexpected tenderness. She didn't remember taking the piece with her, didn't recall tucking it away among her belongings. And yet, here it was, a tangible reminder of Blackwood Manor's haunting, a sliver of the past that had found its way back to her.

As she held the veil in her hands, Mara felt a faint whisper in the back of her mind, a presence she hadn't felt since the night the manor crumbled. It was Seraphina, a quiet echo of the widow's spirit, lingering just beyond reach, like a shadow in the edges of her consciousness. Though the curse had lifted and Blackwood Manor was gone, a part of Seraphina remained—a reminder of the pain she had endured, the regrets she had carried, and the final peace she had found.

For a long moment, Mara sat in silence, her gaze fixed on the veil, her mind filled with memories of the house, the broken love, the betrayal, the sorrow that had bound Seraphina to her fate. She felt a strange comfort in the fragment, a sense of closure that was bittersweet but deeply satisfying.

"Goodbye, Seraphina," she whispered, her voice soft, filled with both compassion and resolve. She understood now that some hauntings would never fully fade, that certain memories left marks that couldn't be erased. But they didn't need to be feared. They were reminders, echoes that carried lessons, memories that shaped who she was.

She folded the veil carefully, placing it in a small box on her dresser. It was a part of her now, a memento of the journey she had taken, of the courage it had taken to confront the darkness within Blackwood Manor and herself. She would carry it with her, not as a haunting, but as a symbol of resilience, a testament to the strength she had found within herself.

That night, as she drifted off to sleep, Mara felt a warmth settle over her, a quiet, peaceful presence that filled her dreams. She saw Seraphina, standing in a field bathed in sunlight, her face free from the bitterness and sorrow that had haunted her in life. The widow looked at her, a soft smile on her lips, her expression filled with gratitude.

"Thank you, Mara," Seraphina's voice whispered, faint but clear, a final, gentle farewell.

Mara awoke with a sense of peace she hadn't known before, her heart light, her spirit unburdened. She knew that she had finally said goodbye, that Seraphina's presence, though lingering in memory, had found peace at last.

And as the morning sun filled her room with warm light, Mara knew that she, too, was free.

Disclaimer for The Widow's Web

This is a work of fiction. Names, characters, places, and incidents are products of the author's imagination or used fictitiously only. Any resemblance to actual persons, living or deceased, businesses, locales, or events is purely coincidental.

This book contains elements of horror, suspense, and supernatural themes that may be unsettling or distressing to some readers. It is intended for mature audiences who are comfortable with stories involving themes of psychological tension, death, and haunting imagery. Reader discretion is advised.

The author does not endorse or promote any real-world practices, beliefs, or rituals depicted within the story. All paranormal and supernatural elements are intended solely for fictional and entertainment purposes.